Without Brakes:

Fingers Crossed

A Collection of Short Stories from Rocky Mountain Fiction Writers

RMFW PRESS

Without Brakes: Fingers Crossed
By Rocky Mountain Fiction Writers
Copyright© 2024 RMFW Press
ISBN Print: 978-1-7345756-5-1

Where the River Ends © 2024 J. Warren Weaver
Beyond Carbon © 2024 Rachel Delaney Craft
The Tamarisk Hunter © 2006 Paolo Bacigalupi
Our Sprinkler System © 2024 Lesley L. Smith
Rightsizing © 2024 Jeff Jaskot
Attack of the Third Planet © 2024 Collin Irish
Iphus © 2024 Laurel McHargue
Visited by a Crane © 2024 Rick Ginsberg
Sticka © 2024 Natasha Watts
The Cistern © 2024 Mark Stevens
Stokes the Happy © 2024 Cepa Onion
We'll Always Have Peaches © 2024 Ryanne Glenn
A Blip in Time © 2024 Patricia Stoltey

All rights reserved. No part of this book may be reproduced or transmitted in any form or by an means, electronic or mechanical, including photocopy, recording, or by any information storage and retrieval system, without permission in writing from the author or his/ her agent, except by a reviewer who may quote brief passages in a critical article or review to be printed in a magazine or newspaper, or electronically transmitted on radio, television, or the Internet.

All persons, places, and organizations in this book except those clearly in the public domain are fictitious, and any resemblance that may exist to actual persons, places, events, or organizations living or dead, or defunct, is purely coincidental. These are works of fiction.

RMFW Press, PO Box 711, Montrose, CO 81402

www.rmfw.org

Cover design by Emir Orucevic

Printed in the United States of America

When the well is dry, we know the worth of water.

Benjamin Franklin

Editors' Note

This anthology began when someone lit fires under our behinds. Literally.

When the Decker fire consumed 6000 acres near Salida, Colorado, nearby flames forced Linda and her husband to evacuate their home. As days passed, with slurry bombers flying overhead, Linda wondered if she would have a home to return to. After the Marshal fire incinerated 1000 structures in suburban Boulder County, Paul and his wife moved a dog, two cats, and carloads of boxes into temporary accommodations to provide housing for victims who had lost their home. Paul was still writing at an ill-fitting desk in the corner of his in-laws' guest room when he and Linda first considered co-editing this anthology.

There could be only one theme, Colorado's Changing Climate.

We asked Rocky Mountain Fiction Writers (RMFW) members to send us page-turning stories with a strong premise, characters embroiled in conflict, rich settings, stunning climaxes, and a tie-in to the theme. Severe climate is commonplace in the Centennial State. It should be equally common in every story of loss, hope, romance, and reconciliation.

RMFW members provided stories that we were proud to include. The authors' creativity and passion are evident throughout. Climate whispered or screamed from every story submitted. Still other authors took advantage of the flexible theme to delight us with creative interpretations.

You're holding the result. In these stories, you'll discover the power of a lie and the devastation of a drought, orchards that wither and love that blossoms, secrets that must be exposed and others that must remain hidden. Action is the only response to a changing climate, and our stories show that even small gestures can make a difference. Each story will impact you in a personal way, just as intense climate events have touched every one of us.

From story selection to publication and marketing, this anthology has been a team effort. We would like to thank our volunteers—Rachel Delaney Craft, Amber Herbert, Laurel McHargue, and Pamela Goldner Prohoroff—for their suggestions, encouragement, and invaluable assistance with judging, editing, and formatting. Thanks also to Susan Brooks, Natasha Christensen, Todd Leatherman, Kelley Lindberg, ZJ Czupor, and many others who provided support and guidance throughout the project.

While we appreciate our entire cast of award-winning and talented authors, we offer our sincere appreciation to Colorado-based, internationally bestselling author Paolo Bacigalupi for including his story in this anthology. His poignant sci-fi contribution, The Tamarisk Hunter, brings to life the consequences of a future with the loss of fresh water on our planet.

As a reflection of the times, RMFW does not allow AI-generated content, (in whole, or in part, including text, images, or translations) to be submitted to RMFW anthologies. All contributing authors have certified that their work is original and no portion has been created using AI. These stories came directly from the minds and hearts of RMFW members. Every word reflects human values, emotions, and experience.

We met as members of RMFW and the Speculative Fiction Writers critique group—two organizations that taught us story structure, the mechanics of self-publishing, and how to use an Oxford comma. We know the value for emerging authors to have their story selected and see it in print. Co-editing is a way for us to give that experience to others, to pay it forward. Throughout the process of judging, editing, production, and promotion, we have grown as editors and writers. We hope you value this anthology as much as we have valued the experience of placing it in your hands.

Colorado's changing climate is an undeniable reality, but so is the imagination of the RMFW community. May these stories open hearts, stir emotions, and light a fire under your collective behinds.

Paul and Linda
Spring 2024

Table of Contents

Editors' Note v

Where the River Ends / *J. Warren Weaver* 1

Beyond Carbon / *Rachel Delaney Craft* 9

The Tamarisk Hunter / *Paolo Bacigalupi* 33

Our Sprinkler System / *Lesley L. Smith* 53

Rightsizing / *Jeff Jaskot* 62

Attack of the Third Planet / *Collin Irish* 76

Iphus / *Laurel McHargue* 93

Visited by a Crane / *Rick Ginsberg* 103

Sticka / *Natasha Watts* 115

The Cistern / *Mark Stevens* 132

Stokes the Happy / *Cepa Onion* 155

We'll Always Have Peaches / *Ryanne Glenn* 166

A Blip in Time / *Pat Stoltey* 174

About the Editors 190

Where the River Ends

J. Warren Weaver

Henry sat on the edge of the rusting old railroad bridge, his legs hanging off the side. The bridge was a relic of another time, another world. It'd never been meant for pedestrians, as evidenced by the lack of safety rails along its soaring sides. The powers that be—the railway's original owners—had let it go into a state of decay after the local coal mining operation closed their doors and left town. It'd been tough times for the small Colorado mountain town, but none of that concerned Henry much as he stretched his legs out over the dying river that snaked by below.

His feet swung back and forth in empty space as hot gusts of wind rasped off the mountaintop and down into the river basin like the breath of some avenging dragon. He watched as the surrounding trees buckled against the sudden onslaughts and wondered if any would topple over and roll into the muddy riverbed below. The beetles had moved through the once-luscious pines years prior, killing everything in their wake, leaving nothing but the bony fingers of skeletons trapped just beneath the surface, forever left trying to claw their way free of their rocky tomb.

He could still remember a time when only the beauty of nature surrounded him. An oasis of exploration and freedom. A forest so lush, he wondered if it'd swallow him whole at times. The area had been filled with so much life, nearly untouched by the machinations of man. It would eventually be labeled "a hidden gem in the Rockies" as the town tried to drum up tourism to fill the void the coal mine had left, and it worked.

All the better for Henry, it turned out.

But back before any of that, before all the changes, when Henry was still young, the sound of birdsong rang out from every direction as statuesque deer paid witness to his methodical movements along the unkempt, overgrown, dirt hiking trails. Back then, he'd been as familiar with the forest as he was with his own face in the mirror. It was his safe place, his refuge. It'd been where he ran to when things needed sorting out, escaping from. When he'd needed to hide.

Fire had taken most of that—the animals, the beauty—and sent it down the road. To where, he wasn't sure he knew. He just hoped that scenic peace, that place filled with the sense of calm he'd so loved, still existed somewhere. That happy place had long since faded for him.

It wasn't the beetles or the drought that had ended it, but they sure didn't help. Not even that fire that'd ripped down the mountainside and claimed three lives in the blink of an eye. No, it'd been gone long before any of that. It'd disappeared during that awkward stage between childhood innocence and an awareness of the cold reality of the world that only adults understand. There's no easing in . . . that change. One day you're a kid, then the next, you simply aren't.

For Henry, it was a series of events that had ushered in that sad understanding of the way things truly were—that'd robbed him of any glimmer of the beauty he'd tried so desperately to cling to. He'd been changed in ways that he still struggled to understand, to cope with. The crucible of his life—a single moment of raw instinct, and it had forever molded him, shaped him into the man he was today.

And today, he was fighting that urge again.

The drying river below him, the mud creeping down from the banks as if it were trying to strangle the rush of water to a slow drip, was a reminder that he had to be careful. A not-so-subtle warning that he had to be smart. When the barrels in Lake Mead started to turn up, well, Henry got a little worried. But that was Nevada. That was the desert. He was in the mountains. And he'd always been cautious. He'd considered every factor he could think of, but he'd never factored that the once rushing river below might become little more than the sad trickle it was today.

It'd taken years of mismanagement for the reservoir to drop to a historic low, according to the news. But it was much more recently that the dock had settled into the mud, that even the mud had started to dry and crack up closer to the shoreline. Henry had never fathomed that the reservoir, so full and teeming with life, so immense and seemingly endless, would shrink to match the dark deposits he'd made so many times in the dead of night. It was only a matter of time before they found something other than the rotting carcasses of the fish that'd been trapped in the shallow, quickly evaporating pools of water.

It was only a matter of time before they found the first body.

Henry wondered how it'd look, who it'd be. Would it just be the skeletal remains of his first victim? That evil man that'd forced himself on Henry over and over again, his unwanted touch a nightly nightmare. Doing it again and again until even Henry's happy place dissolved like a salted slug, until he'd snapped, his mind gone primal. No more flight, only fight. Would it be that sinister man, that predator?

He thought back to the horror in his mother's eyes, her disbelief finally erased as she rushed into the room and found Henry's stepfather gurgling his last gasps through the hole in his throat Henry had made in his desperate attempt to escape the man's sweaty, ham-fisted advances. The booze still thick on his breath, leaking from his oily pores.

His mother had to pry the bloody pocketknife from Henry's grip as the effects of shock sent his mind to a different place and made his whole body go rigid as rigor mortis, while the skinny man gushed blood all over him. His mother had been the one to think of dumping the body into the reservoir. The family had a rowboat there, old as the coal mines, but still water-worthy.

That was back when the parking lot was still dirt, back before they'd gated it and thrown a chain-link fence along the perimeter. It'd taken every bit of strength for the two of them to pull that lanky body into the bed of the beat-up truck, their hearts racing with every odd noise that pierced the silent night. They'd reclaimed some old cinder blocks from the trees out behind the house and chained them around the man's bony ankles before pushing him overboard.

Henry would never forget the sound of his passage—hardly even a splash. It was more of a deep gurgle as the water opened wide and accepted him. His mother had cried, holding her only son close as the pale form of her former lover—his tormentor—disappeared into the dark murk below. People disappear in those mountains all the time, they agreed.

"You must never tell a soul what we done here tonight," she'd warned him, and he'd listened.

But something broke in him that night, something no amount of therapy could fix. He felt like the devil had crawled into that space between youth and manhood and made himself comfortable. The devil had spent four decades making that spot his own.

He was there to stay.

Henry was deep in thought when the crunch of gravel behind him nearly sent him plummeting to his death below. The firm grip on his shoulder was the only thing that kept him on that rickety iron bridge.

"Jesus Christ!" he managed as his eyes raced to find who had snuck up on him so easily.

"Don' chu have a heart attack, ol' man!"

Mark. Thank God.

"Nearly sent me into the river, Mark!"

"Well, you was looking so peaceful I didn't wanna disturb ya. More just wanted to join in and see what it was you's was looking at down there."

"Just trying to see the past, I suppose," Henry responded after he managed to calm his racing heart, bring his breath back to normal.

"Now, what in the hell is that s'pose to mean?"

Henry smiled. He couldn't help it. Mark was a simple man. Probably why Henry liked him. There was something about the truly dumb that gave Henry comfort. Maybe it was because he never needed to worry that they'd see through his façade.

"Remember when this thing used to be raging? Back when it was full?"

"I sure do," Mark responded, his long legs stretching toward the land below as he joined Henry on the edge of the bridge. "I caught many a fish in them waters growin' up. Almost drowned a time or two when it was floodin' the banks. My brother bet me I couldn't swim it. Proved him wrong."

"I'm sure you did," Henry said, allowing himself to reflect on better times for a moment before his worries reached back out and caressed his mind, sending a shiver down his spine. "But it's all gone now. Just left with the memories."

"If you say so. For a minute there, I was wonderin' you spotted somethin' down there in the mud, just like that gal over at the reservoir."

Henry's blood ran cold, and it must have shown because Mark's smile disappeared like the morning mist in the summer sun.

"You okay, Henry? You havin' one of them heart attacks or somethin'?"

Henry did his best to shake off the sinking feeling that beckoned him to jump from that bridge and get it over with.

Do it, said the devil in the back of his head.

He shook the thought loose and turned to regard Mark's worried face.

"Just a little light-headed all of a sudden. Low blood sugar. Skipped breakfast this morning."

"You shouldn't do that. Momma told me it's the most important meal of the day," Mark said, his face suddenly serious.

"Your momma's a smart lady." Henry had to smother his grin so as not to offend the man. He was a bit touchy when it came to his mother. "You said they found something at the reservoir?"

"They sure did!" Mark's face lit up with the joy of a child at a carnival. "Sheriff's pretty hush-hush on it, but I heard tell it's a body."

Jump. Just end it, the devil reiterated, his voice a whispering rasp.

"A body? Well, wouldn't that be something?" Henry's eyes went back to the dying river below, and he found himself calculating the distance between them.

"Probably one of them kids that drowned, would be my guess."

"Might be," Henry responded.

So it had started. He'd known it was coming. He'd been trying to prepare himself, but nothing hit as hard and with as much force as reality. They'd found a body. One of his victims. Now he had to play the waiting game. Which body? From what decade?

He'd gotten better at covering up his crimes, as his life deviated further down that sinister path. The cinder blocks became weighted backpacks. He'd steal them from vacant campsites, the occupants out exploring the wonders of nature. No one was the wiser. Hikers lost things all the time, and he was always sure to stay out of sight.

He focused his urges on the less desirable—the transients. No one missed them enough to report their disappearance. Low-hanging fruit, as the saying went. But on occasion, when the urge got too bad and the devil wouldn't let him be still, he'd lose all inhibition . . . if they found one of those victims, Henry was in for it. People already had a sense about him, the smart ones anyway.

Yep, the Sheriff would surely want to talk with him. It was only a matter of time.

Just end it. Jump, the devil screeched, seeing Henry's destiny as clearly as the man himself did.

Was there still the death penalty in this state? He really couldn't remember—things had changed so much in his lifetime. Did it matter? How many times had he listened to the devil and given in to that urge?

That urge to do evil.

"Think they'll find more bodies, like they been doin' up at that lake in Nevada?" Mark's question broke Henry out of his dark, swirling thoughts.

"Were I a betting man, I'd say yes."

But only you know how many, the devil cackled.

Henry looked around at all the dying things surrounding him and smiled. How fitting. All he could do now was wait.

Or just end it . . .

J. Warren Weaver is the award-winning author of the *Shadow of a Spy* trilogy. His second installment, A *Killer of Spies*, was the 2023 CIPA Evvy gold medal winner for the thrillers/suspense category. Weaver lives a charmed life in small town Colorado, where he enjoys the bountiful great outdoors with his wife, baby girl, and their three mischievous dogs. When not playing the clown for his daughter, he tries to find the time to write page-turning thrillers that'll have you up all night, looking over your shoulder, questioning everything you thought you already knew.

Beyond Carbon

Rachel Delaney Craft

When "Dan Marez" showed up for his first day on the job, it wasn't a security guard or HR rep who greeted him.

"I'm Natalie Sykes," the woman said, shaking his hand firmly. "President and CEO of Beyond Carbon."

Even if "Dan Marez," whose real name was Daniel Herrera Jr., weren't an investigative reporter who'd been digging up dirt on this company for three months before going undercover, he would have heard of Natalie Sykes. She was all over the internet these days, the latest poster child of the climate fight.

"I know who you are, ma'am," Dan said, laying the accent on thick. He'd grown up in Colorado Springs, but he could flawlessly adopt his father's accent when he needed to—it made people like Sykes see him as less of a threat. "You are a great inventor. You made the . . . the new fans, right?"

Sykes didn't blush, or even smile. Instead, a cloud passed over the sky blue of her eyes as she led him into a polished conference room.

"Yes, I invented a new kind of fan to capture carbon from the atmosphere. It can draw ten times as much as conventional carbon capture methods. This is a pilot facility, a place to test the fans and prove the technology before we start scaling it up."

She waved an elegant hand toward the conference room window. Beyond the glass, the massive fans could be seen sucking carbon out of the air and churning it down into the rocks beneath the prairie, its final resting place.

Brushing prematurely gray curls from her face, Sykes slid a sheet of paper across the table.

"This is a non-disclosure agreement. A lot of legalese, so don't worry about reading every word."

This statement would have insulted any reporter on a molecular level—but, Dan reminded himself, Sykes thought he was a custodian who'd dropped out of high school. He let his eyes widen as he looked over the densely typed paragraphs.

"It boils down to this," Sykes explained. "You can't discuss anything you see or hear during your employment with anyone outside the company."

In the time she'd spent translating for him, Dan had skimmed the entire page, and even caught two grammatical errors. It was the standard NDA verbiage—until he reached the last paragraph.

"What's this?" he asked, frowning at the words.

"Ah. That's one of our ground rules here at Beyond Carbon. The only one, really."

He looked up at her, his clueless expression slipping slightly. "I can't work . . . after dark?"

He checked the paper again to ensure he'd read the words right. It didn't say he had to work a certain shift or clock in at a certain time. It said: *Employees are not to be within the facility gates outside of daylight hours. Failure to comply may be grounds for termination.*

"It may seem arbitrary, Mr. Marez. But I take my employees' health and safety very seriously."

The litany of deaths that had piled up—and been settled out of court—since Beyond Carbon opened two years ago suggested otherwise, Dan thought. But he couldn't let on that he knew anything about this.

"I know the reputation startup companies have," Sykes went on. "I want Beyond Carbon to be different. I want my employees to have a healthy work-life balance so they'll stay with me. Save the world with me. That's why you'll start with six weeks of vacation, unlimited sick time, comped health insurance—and reasonable hours. To facilitate this, the gate will be locked from sunset to sunrise."

Dan couldn't help looking mildly incredulous. In his fifteen years investigating stories like this one, he'd met plenty of control freaks, micromanagers, and tyrannical startup dictators. But this? For about the millionth time over the last few months, he wished Elise hadn't dumped him. He wished he had a roommate, or even a cat—*anyone* to talk to about this bizarre rule when he got home.

"Are you comfortable with these conditions, Mr. Marez?" Sykes asked, rapping a pen on the paper.

"Oh, yes. Yes, ma'am." Dan took the pen and scrawled his fake name.

Every story was important—too important, if you asked Elise. But ever since he'd started researching Beyond Carbon's employee deaths, this one had felt more mysterious than usual. He had a feeling it could be big. Explosive. Career-making.

"Welcome to the team," Sykes said as Dan handed the paper back.

"Looking forward to it."

His heart ticked a little faster in his ribcage. It always did when the hunt was on.

Dan's supervisor was a small woman named Vicky, who smelled like an ashtray and looked vaguely like a gargoyle. She showed him around the building: the custodians' break room, the closet full of cleaning supplies, the riding floor waxer.

She patted it fondly. "This here's John Deere."

"Did you have to sign that form?" Dan asked, unable to contain his curiosity any longer. "About not working at night?"

He didn't want to raise any suspicions on his first day, but the NDA's after-dark clause was so odd, it would be suspicious *not* to ask about it.

Vicky sniffed. "We all did, a few months back. Before that, we worked the night shift, like normal janitors."

"Why'd you stop?"

The leathery skin on Vicky's face worked itself into a strange expression. "Listen. Whatever corn Sykes fed you about work-life balance, don't buy it. The night rule is a safety thing, plain and simple."

"Safety?" he asked slowly. "What does that mean?"

"It means if you want to live as long as I have, stay out of here after dark. And stay away from those fans."

Standing in the closet doorway, Dan glanced over his shoulder at the nearest window. The fans looked back at him, rows of black eyes in a metal frame, spinning implacably.

"The . . . fans?"

With a terse smile, Vicky shoved a mop into his hands. "Show me what you can do with this. Impress me, and I just might hand over the keys to this baby." She jerked a thumb at John Deere.

"What about the fans?" Dan pressed. "Are they dangerous?"

"Can't tell you." She shook her head sadly, as if it weren't her decision.

"I should know if I'm going to work here."

"I can't tell you," she said again, "because you'd never believe me. Now, get to mopping."

Dan didn't want to draw attention by asking too many questions. For the first couple of weeks he lay low, mopping, sweeping, and vacuuming until his hands were raw. He worked hard to fit in with the other custodians, to build rapport with his coworkers. He brought in donuts every Friday to facilitate the rapport part.

It was funny, the things you learned. Like the fact that Vicky was the only custodian who'd been here the entire two years. After her, Lamar had been here the longest, and he'd only graduated high school last spring. Pretty high turnover rate for a company that prided itself on work-life balance. Or that once a month, the custodians had to clean the mysterious fans—a task that no one seemed to talk about. They complained about dusting Sykes's office and joked about scrubbing toilets, but when Dan asked about the fans, everyone went quiet.

At night, in the emptiness of his Denver apartment, Dan pored over his notes on the glowing screen of his laptop. Vicky's dates lined up. There had been no accidents at

Beyond Carbon in the last three months, since Sykes implemented the after-dark policy. Before that, there was little public information about the six deaths. Dan had hunted down girlfriends, boyfriends, siblings, parents. One had cited an electrical accident; another had mentioned burns. The rest didn't seem to know how their loved ones had died.

That was the pattern Dan had looked for when he began his research: a common cause of death. But the only pattern that had emerged was the general lack of information.

So he scoured his notes for a new one, occasionally jotting his thoughts on a pad of paper. He couldn't help glancing up at the armchair where Elise used to sit, her legs folded beneath her, typing up her latest autopsy report. She had always been good at spotting patterns. She was trained to look for them, just in flesh and blood rather than data.

With a sigh, Dan tore his gaze away from the chair and scraped the last of his cold Pad Thai from its plastic takeout tray. Then he glanced down at his freshly scrawled notes.

Victims
3 security guards on night shift
2 custodians who worked nights
1 engineer w/ habit of staying late

Whatever was happening at Beyond Carbon, it only happened after dark. And he suspected it had something to do with those fans.

Sinking back in his chair, he rubbed his weary eyes and glanced at the photo perched on the corner of the desk. Him around age ten, wrapped in his father's arms. They were both smiling—at each other, not the camera. Dan had just climbed a tree and been too scared to come down. Papá had told him to jump. He said he would catch him, and he did.

The image had faded over the last two and a half decades, but Dan's memory filled in the missing details. Like his dad's fingernails, perpetually blackened with machine shop grime. Or the empty place on his right hand where his pinky had been lost to a table saw. For his dad, every day meant another twelve hours of sweating and hunching and sucking metal dust. For Dan, it meant another day worrying that his father might come home in pieces.

His gaze darted back to the laptop screen, to the words *electrical accident*. Turns out he'd been worrying about the wrong danger lurking in that machine shop.

What if that turned out to be the danger lurking behind this story, too? What if those mysterious fans weren't grounded right, just like the CNC that had killed Daniel Herrera Sr.?

"Tomorrow's fan cleaning day," he murmured, turning back to his dad's face. Not that he believed in ghosts. He wished he could believe in heaven, like his father had, but this job had made him too cynical for that. "I'm going to get to the bottom of this, Papá."

Cleaning the fans was an all-day, all-team job. There were three rows, stacked on top of each other, each one taller than a person. To reach them, Dan had to climb the stairs and walk down the long platform behind the fans. It was perfectly safe, walled in by the fans on one side and a chest-high railing on the other. Still, a shudder ran through him. Maybe it was because the usually humming fans had been shut down for the day, so the place was enveloped in silence.

Maybe it was the way the metal floor clattered, echoing in the still air.

Maybe it was knowing that six people had died here.

"First you gotta take out the filters," his partner Lamar explained as he unlatched a massive metal panel behind the nearest fan. It swung open to reveal a grid of filters, each about three feet square and clogged with reddish brown dust, gravel, and squashed grasshoppers.

Lamar lifted out the first one, revealing part of the fan. Through a twisted gap between the blades, a sliver of desert showed beyond. Dan reached for another filter.

Lamar's head snapped up. "Not like that. Hold 'em by the sides. Don't touch the spongy stuff."

Frowning, Dan gripped the filter's cardboard frame and eased it from its slot. He followed Lamar's lead and dropped it into a box marked HAZMAT.

"Is it, like, a cleanliness thing?"

"Nah," Lamar said. "It'll just give you a little shock. Look."

He pulled out the next filter with practiced ease and held it up to the sunlight, tilting it slightly to give Dan a better look. It took a moment to spot the flicker of electricity passing over the filter material. It was similar to the static that crackled through his fleece blanket when he took it out of the dryer, except instead of white, this spark looked almost green. Instead of flickering and zigzagging across the fabric, it curled and rippled.

"Huh. Why don't they get different filters?"

Lamar shrugged as he dropped it in the box. "They've tried. It's not the filter—it's something in the air. Something about the dust out here, I guess."

Dan frowned at the hazmat box. "Is that why they can't

go in a trash bag like everything else?"

"Guess so." Once they had removed all the filters, Lamar clicked the lid shut. "Sometimes the engineers ask for a couple, for their 'research.' Rest of 'em end up in the incinerator."

Before they put fresh filters in, Lamar showed Dan how to clean the fan blades using what looked like a shop vac on steroids. He pressed the long tube through one of the openings where the filters used to be and navigated it between the blades.

"You hold that steady." Lamar pointed to the vacuum's base, then cracked a grin. "Now, switch me on and watch the master at work."

Dan pressed the power button, and the vacuum roared to life. Lamar began moving the tube skillfully around the giant metal curves of the blades. The more Dan watched, the more he saw the strange flickers of electricity—crackling between the blades, jumping off the edge of the tube, rippling inside the vacuum's wide barrel as it collected dust.

So far, the mystery of Beyond Carbon seemed relatively simple. Everything pointed to electricity. But ever since he'd seen his father's body in 12th grade—ever since he'd dedicated his life to toppling careless companies like Beyond Carbon and negligent CEOs like Sykes—Dan had learned a lot about electricity. And something about this made the hairs on the back of his neck prickle.

A sound interrupted Dan's thoughts. A hum, barely audible over the whirr of the vacuum. He strained his ears. A distant buzzing, like flies gathering over a piece of roadkill—

With a start, he realized it wasn't flies. It was voices. The more he listened, the more the sounds shaped themselves into words. Countless words, in countless voices, weaving and overlapping and crashing against each other.

"Dan man?"

Lamar's voice jolted him back to reality, and he realized Lamar had turned off the vacuum. He stood in front of Dan, the vacuum tube hefted over one shoulder, like a custodial lumberjack.

"You heard 'em," Lamar said. It wasn't a question.

Dan shook his head. Talking made it easier to tune out the voices, but they never quite went away. They were always there, lurking in the background.

"Jesus. Feels like I'm losing my mind."

"Right? Like, at first you don't notice 'em. But once you do, you can't stop."

"What the hell is it?" Dan asked.

Lamar shrugged. "No one knows. No one really *wants* to know. But I hear it gets worse at night. Vicky told me back in the day, people could barely get through the vacuuming without screaming."

Dan frowned. The way people talked around here, he felt like he was in the opening scenes of some low-budget horror movie.

"Creepy, right?" Lamar glanced up at the clear blue sky, where the sun was steadily sinking toward the horizon. "Now let's get this over with so we can go home before dark."

Dan looked down at the vacuum's transparent dust barrel, flickering with the occasional pale green light.

"Creepy," he murmured, and flipped the switch back on.

As Lamar resumed vacuuming, Dan tried to ignore the sinking feeling in his stomach. He couldn't fall for any of the custodians' superstitions. He'd built his career on cold, hard facts—and that was what he needed to untangle this bizarre story.

Which meant he would have to work late that night.

It wasn't hard to surreptitiously stay late. Once the fans were clean, the custodians scattered with the air of cops who'd just gotten off duty at a particularly grisly crime scene.

Dan understood. Even when he returned to the building, out of earshot of the fans, the strange voices seemed to have wormed into his skull. He felt a headache brewing, and he wanted nothing more than to crash on his couch with a bowl of instant ramen. Instead, he busied himself re-cleaning one of the bathrooms until the building emptied and the overhead lights dimmed. Then he gathered his lunchbox and keys.

When he reached the front desk, one of the guards looked up, alarmed. His badge said KEVIN KHAN.

"Why are you still here?" he asked.

Dan followed Kevin's gaze out the wide glass double doors, where the last dregs of sunlight winked through the cracks between the enormous fans.

"It's not quite dark yet," Dan said. "What's that rule for, anyway?"

The other guard glanced up from filing her nails. "You'll see when you go outside."

"See what?"

Kevin hmphed at his partner, then glanced at his watch. "Two more minutes, then I'll have to write you up."

"See what?" Dan asked again.

The other guard shook her head. "You wouldn't believe me if I told you."

Her words actually gave Dan the shivers—because Vicky had said the same thing.

Kevin twitched. "One minute and forty-eight—"

Dan didn't need to be told twice. He was already shouldering his lunchbox and pushing through the doors.

It was still warm out; the desert didn't really cool off until well past sunset, even in October. A breeze blew past Dan's face, rattling the dry brown rosebushes planted along the walkway to the parking lot. On one side, headlights flicked past on the highway he would take to get home. On the other, flat yellow earth stretched away, interrupted only by prairie dog mounds and the towering grid of fans.

Dan wasn't sure what he was supposed to look for, but he knew it had something to do with those fans.

He paused by his hail-dented Subaru and looked up. In the twilight, strange lights flickered against the fans' hulking silhouettes. They were wispy and silvery green, just like the sparks he'd seen on the filters. But they were bigger, and they seemed to grow more solid with each passing moment.

He stepped closer. The longer he looked, the more the lights took shape. He could almost imagine the top part as a head, the bottom part splitting off into arms and legs—but that was just a trick of his eyes, right? Just the natural human inclination to turn meaningless shapes into faces?

"Hey!" A voice behind him made Dan turn. Kevin the security guard stood in the open doorway, waving a piece of paper. "Do you want me to write you up?"

With an apologetic wave, Dan opened the car door and climbed into the driver's seat. But before he pulled out of the lot, he took out his phone and snapped a quick picture.

Once he got through the gate—where another guard reprimanded him—and back to his apartment, he took out his phone to examine the photo. To make sure he wasn't crazy.

There were the fans, a black rectangle against the dim orange-streaked sky. The lights were gone.

The following Saturday, Dan paid a visit to an old friend at the coroner's office. "Friend" wasn't really an accurate label for Elise, unless you added the words "ex" and "girl" in front of it. In all Dan's research before going undercover, this was the one lead he hadn't yet followed.

Elise was wrist-deep in the vital organs of some poor soul who must have died under suspicious circumstances—at least, suspicious enough to warrant a weekend autopsy. When Dan cleared his throat, she spun around. Her expression started with surprise, then passed through something harder to define before landing on annoyance. She fixed him with a glare.

"Guess you survived that last undercover assignment," she said, as if this were a disappointment. "Bringing down—Who was it? America's biggest soybean farm?"

He gave a rueful nod. That was the story that had ended this particular relationship. "I got a big promotion for it."

"Good for you," she said flatly. "What the hell do you want?"

"Oh, you know." He joined her at the table, glad the receptionist had given him some menthol cream for his upper lip. "Just wanted to see how you're doing."

"It's amazing how you can fool those corporate idiots,

but somehow I can always tell when you're lying. Spit it out."

Dan smiled despite himself. "What do you know about the Beyond Carbon employee deaths?"

Behind her glasses, Elise's deep brown eyes widened. "*That's* your story? Good luck. Natalie Sykes got all those records sealed up tighter than a dolphin's—"

"I know." He did his best not to look at the slabs of skin lying open on the table. "But you must have seen the victims. You must have worked on at least one of them."

Her lips pressed together. She went quiet—just like Dan's new coworkers when he'd brought up the fans.

"A couple," she said finally.

"And? How'd they look?" Dan wondered what kind of grisly wounds could make someone like Elise squirm.

"Weird. Just . . . weird." She peeled off her bloody gloves and dropped them into a red bio-waste bin, then massaged her forehead.

"Did it have anything to do with electricity?"

Her eyebrows lifted. She leaned forward, her eyes sparkling with that old familiar light, and Dan could almost imagine they had never broken up. "The only marks on them were two burns."

He nodded, memories of his father's body flashing before his eyes. "Entry and exit wounds."

"Except when people electrocute themselves, the entry wound is usually where they touched the voltage source—most often a hand. Sometimes the armpits, because sweat is so conductive. These entry wounds were in the middle of the chest."

"What about lightning?"

Elise shook her head. "Lightning almost never leaves

marks. But here's the weirdest part. The exit wounds looked normal—big black spot on the sole of the foot. But the entry wounds, on the chest? They were shaped like *this*." She held up her palm, fingers spread. "Like a *handprint*. That's why the medical report never went public. We didn't want to start rumors about aliens and whatnot—we get enough of that shit out here."

Dan steadied himself on the metal table. Burns shaped like palm prints? Electricity shaped like vague human forms that didn't show up on camera? This story was straight out of a conspiracy theory. Pretty soon, mutilated cattle would start turning up in the fields around Beyond Carbon.

"Dan? You okay?"

He blinked back to reality. Suddenly Elise was very close, head tilted, concern etched in her heart-shaped face.

"Yeah. It's just . . . it's just this . . . "

"*This story.*" She stepped back, her cold expression snapping back into place. "How many times have I heard that before?"

"This one's different," he said quietly. "It's making me feel like . . . like I'm losing it. Like I'm seeing ghosts."

Elise studied him for a moment. "Why did you come to me?"

"Like you said. The records were sealed tighter than—"

"No, I mean why *me*? Why not one of my colleagues?"

Dan paused. "I don't know. Why didn't you tell me to get lost and ask one of your colleagues instead?"

"I don't know."

Silence filled the distance between them. Dan didn't particularly want to leave—maybe because of Elise, or maybe because he didn't want to go home and email his editor about the absurd direction this story was going.

Then he remembered the photo on his desk. His father had never quit anything in his life.

"Thanks for your help," he said and headed for the door.

To avoid raising suspicion, Dan waited three weeks before trying to catch another glimpse of the strange phenomenon in the fans. He spent that time blowing off his editor and doing something that deeply ashamed every fiber of his being: He researched ghosts. Specifically, how to capture them on camera.

He ventured into the nuttiest corners of the internet. He scoured Craigslist, buying odd things from odd people who probably shouldn't be trusted with his credit card information. He built a "spirit-cam," as they seemed to be called, with a special type of film and fancy polymer-coated lens. He wouldn't know if it worked until he got the film developed, but it was worth a try.

He knew he wouldn't get past the security guards a second time, so he took a different approach. He drove to Beyond Carbon after nightfall, parked on the side of the highway, and walked the rest of the way. He used a headlamp to navigate the dark prairie, and bolt cutters to get through the fence.

Was it a felony? Yes. Would his editor be happy? She'd probably have a stroke. But Dan knew how far people like Sykes would go to cover up their transgressions. If her guards caught him in the act, he'd have bigger fish to fry than the judicial system.

He set his jaw as he approached the fans. There came a time in every case when you had to take the plunge to reach the final clue, the last scrap of evidence that would break the story wide open. This was it.

Even from this distance, he could make out the shapes sparking against the night sky, curling between the spinning fan blades. He could hear them, too. Whispers, murmurs, questions. The voices burrowed into his skull, muddling his thoughts, fraying his nerves.

The door to the stairs had a light-sensitive lock, so he wouldn't be able to get up close and personal with the ghosts—if that's what they were. But he had no intention of getting closer. Their strange energy had already killed at least six people, and Dan was determined not to become number seven. He stopped within ten yards of the fans, then raised the clunky contraption hanging around his neck. He tried to keep his hands steady, but the voices made it hard to concentrate.

That's when he realized the voices were growing louder. And the flickering shapes weren't just in the fans anymore—they coiled over the maintenance walkway, spilled onto the ground, drifted toward him. They didn't quite hover the way ghosts did in movies. Their feet always touched the ground, translucent toes dragging over rocks and cacti. Their voices continued to rise, but their mouths didn't move. Like they weren't actually talking. Instead, they seemed to be replaying slivers of memories from their former lives.

Some of them might have been happy memories. But the loudest ones, the ones that blotted out the others, were full of anguish. Someone shouted. Another screamed. A small, young voice sobbed over and over, a moment of childhood grief played on repeat.

Dan shook his head to clear it, but the voices crashed against his skull like a tidal wave. They seemed to paralyze him. Moving was difficult; thinking was nearly impossible. It was time to get the hell out.

But as he turned, still gripping the spirit-cam, another shape pushed its way to the front of the mass of crackling green light. There were many details that could have clued Dan in to its identity: the prematurely stooped shoulders, the right hand with its four wispy fingers instead of five. But that wasn't how he knew. He knew by the way it looked at him.

"Papá," he whispered.

As the ghosts and their voices pressed in around him, Dan sensed, deep in the back of his mind, that he should go. But how could he when his dad was standing right there? He had to talk to him, find his voice in the endless tide, tell him how sorry he was. All his sacrifices had been for Dan, and he needed to know that Dan had spent his life trying to make up for it—

"What are you doing?"

The new voice cut through the others—sharper, louder, more alive. Another figure appeared from behind Dan, the dark silhouette of a living, breathing person.

It wasn't a security guard. It was Natalie Sykes, waving what looked like a lighter.

The orange flame streaked through the darkness. The ghosts crackled and moved back, just an inch or two. With her other hand, Sykes grabbed Dan's arm and pulled him at a run toward the building.

"What were you thinking?" she panted as they ran together clumsily, stumbling over rocks and prairie dog mounds.

What *had* he been thinking? The story was what had brought him here in the first place—always the story. But his dad's ghost was what had made him linger, despite the danger.

He threw a glance back over his shoulder. The group of ghosts followed them, stretching out from the fans like a giant radioactive finger. He could no longer make out his father's shape among them. Had it really been him? Or was he just another random ghostly figure, twisted into Daniel Herrera Sr. by Dan's hopeful imagination?

Sykes swiped her badge at the front door, pushed Dan inside, and dragged him into the conference room where they had first met.

"They're drawn to life," she explained breathlessly. "They sense your heart beating in your chest. During the day, they're just little flickers of energy. But at night, they can take shape. Move around. Go after you."

Even when the door was shut and he was firmly seated in one of the ergonomic chairs, Dan couldn't stop staring at the pale shapes slowly retreating beyond the window.

"They can't walk through walls, thank god," Sykes added.

"Where'd they come from?"

"We're still trying to figure it out," she replied, "which is hard when they're so dangerous. We think they're just floating around the atmosphere. They seem to need a substrate to take shape, though—that's why they're not visible until they enter the fans."

"But there are other carbon capture companies. Why wouldn't they have the same problem?"

"My fans are better. Ten times better. More air, more ghosts." She studied him with her steely eyes. Her perfectly controlled veneer had loosened. Her curls were askew, her chest still heaving beneath her designer blouse. "What are you, a cop?"

"Journalist."

She grunted. "I should've known when you 'accidentally' worked late that day. Nobody works late when the CEO tells them they could lose their job over it. It's an easy rule to follow."

Dan shrugged. "I had to get to the bottom of it."

"Well, here you are," she said sourly. "This low enough for you?"

"It's certainly . . . not what I expected."

"Because it could rock the world of science. Ghosts? *Real* ghosts? If anyone found out—if you had enough hard evidence to convince them—Beyond Carbon would turn into a circus. Everyone would want to see them, talk to them, ask them about the afterlife." She shook her head. "The world doesn't have time for that. We can study ghosts all we want *after* we clean up the atmosphere. For now, my scientists are just trying to make our fans safe so we can scale up our technology and make a difference in the climate fight."

For the first time in their conversation, Dan turned away from the window and studied Sykes's face.

"This isn't about money, is it?" he asked quietly.

A crease formed between her eyebrows. "Of course not. It's about saving the world—which I can't do if my workers keep dying."

"Hence the after-dark rule."

"And the automatic locks, and incinerating the filters. All that's left is a way to suppress them, to keep them from leaving the fans at night." She rattled the lighter in one hand. "Fire works, but in the desert, open flames are obviously a no-go. And we've found artificial lights don't cut it. But there are other ways to constrain them."

Dan thought back. "I've heard silver helps, and iron."

She lifted an eyebrow. "You've done your research. Turns out some of the old myths are true. We've got new parts coming in next week—silver-coated steel. Once we replace the old aluminum platforms and stairs, Beyond Carbon might finally be safe." She glanced meaningfully at the hodgepodge of a camera dangling from Dan's neck. "For as long as we stay in business, that is."

Dan blinked. When he'd started this job, he would have expected her to bribe him, threaten him, maybe even be willing to hurt him to cover up what was going on at Beyond Carbon. And he'd given her the perfect opportunity. She could have easily left him to his fate out on the prairie, among the ghosts.

Instead, she'd saved his life.

Now she was, it seemed, asking him to stop digging. To bury what he knew in favor of the *greater good*. To let her save the world—or at least let her try.

He opened his mouth, but no words came out.

"You don't have to decide now," Sykes said quickly. "Sleep on it—"

Movement out the window startled them. The ghosts had retreated until they were just smears of greenish light against the fans in the distance, but one remained.

Daniel Herrera Sr. pressed a hand to the window—and this time, Dan was sure it was him. Because his outstretched palm was still marked by the electric current that had killed him.

Beside Dan, Sykes rose from her chair. "Wow. I've never seen one so . . . aware."

Dan stepped forward to press his hand against his

father's, a sheet of glass separating them.

"How'd you—" He shook his head. What were the odds of *this* ghost, one among millions floating in the air, getting sucked into Natalie Sykes's fans on this particular day? No. He didn't believe in that much coincidence.

"You've been here a while, haven't you?" he said, his voice shrinking. "You've been . . . waiting for me?"

The eyes, nothing more than dark smudges in the face, didn't blink. But he thought he saw a hazy nod.

"You knew I'd end up here someday. With all the deaths."

The familiar ghostly hum returned—but only one voice this time, cutting through the silence of the conference room.

"Just jump," said a man's voice.

Then a child's, small and shrill: "I'm scared."

"I'll catch you. Let go."

The last words echoed in Dan's ears, growing fainter each time. *Let go. Let go.*

When he looked up, his father had stepped back from the glass. His body rose with almost imperceptible slowness, the heels lifting off the ground, then the soles of the feet, until the only things tethering him here were the tips of his flickering toes.

He raised his scarred hand in goodbye. Then his connection to the ground broke, and he vanished into the night air.

A month later, a knock sounded on Dan's apartment door. He got up from his desk—now officially his home office— to answer it.

"Why'd you want me to come over?" Elise asked.

Dan shrugged as he held the door open for her. "Why'd you say yes?"

She scowled, then glanced around. "Your apartment's less grungy than I remembered."

"I've spruced it up a bit. Had some extra time on my hands, since I lost my job."

She looked up at him sharply. "What happened?"

"I blew my last story. Couldn't dig up anything useful on Beyond Carbon."

"God, I'm sorry. That job was your life."

"It's okay. I've been trying some new stuff—freelance work, magazines."

She narrowed her eyes. "Do you need a CAT scan?"

"I'm trying, El. Really." He glanced at the desk in the corner, the two photos sitting side by side. One showed a man holding a boy in his arms. The other didn't even look real. Just a blur of green light, a sea of shapeless faces. And, at the front, a vaguely familiar one.

"I'm trying to let go," Dan said.

Elise studied him for a long moment. Then her mouth curled upward into the barest ghost of a smile.

Rachel Delaney Craft writes young adult, middle grade, and speculative fiction. She has contributed to three of RMFW's anthologies, and she co-edited the 2020 anthology, *Wild: Uncivilized Tales*, a finalist for the Colorado Book Award. Her short stories have appeared in places like *Cricket*, *Uncharted*, and *Cast of Wonders*, and her novels have won the Colorado Gold and Zebulon Contests. Rachel's stories are often inspired by the foothills of Colorado, where she lives with her partner and two slobbery dogs. Find her on Twitter @RDCwrites or at racheldelaneycraft.com.

First published June 26, 2006 in *High Country News*

The Tamarisk Hunter

Paolo Bacigalupi

In the desert Southwest of 2030 Big Daddy Drought runs the show, California claims all the water, and a water tick named Lolo ekes out a rugged living removing tamarisk.

A big tamarisk can suck 73,000 gallons of river water a year. For $2.88 a day, plus water bounty, Lolo rips tamarisk all winter long.

Ten years ago, it was a good living. Back then, tamarisk shouldered up against every riverbank in the Colorado River Basin, along with cottonwoods, Russian olives, and elms. Ten years ago, towns like Grand Junction and Moab thought they could still squeeze life from a river.

Lolo stands on the edge of a canyon, Maggie the camel his only companion. He stares down into the deeps. It's an hour's scramble to the bottom. He ties Maggie to a juniper and starts down, boot-skiing a gully. A few blades of green grass sprout neon around him, piercing juniper-tagged snow clods. In the late winter, there is just a beginning surge of water down in the deeps; the ice is off the river edges. Up high, the mountains still wear their ragged snow mantles. Lolo smears through mud and hits a channel of scree, sliding and scattering rocks. His jugs of tamarisk poison gurgle and slosh on his back. His shovel and rockbar snag on occasional junipers as he skids by. It will be a long hike out. But then, that's what makes this patch so perfect. It's a long way down, and the riverbanks are largely hidden.

It's a living; where other people have dried out and blown away, he has remained: a tamarisk hunter, a water tick, a stubborn bit of weed. Everyone else has been blown off the land as surely as dandelion seeds, set free to fly south or east, or most of all north where watersheds sometimes still run deep and where even if there are no more lush ferns or deep cold fish runs, at least there is still water for people.

Eventually, Lolo reaches the canyon bottom. Down in the cold shadows, his breath steams.

He pulls out a digital camera and starts shooting his proof. The Bureau of Reclamation has gotten uptight about proof. They want different angles on the offending tamarisk, they want each one photographed before and after, the whole process documented, GPS'd, and uploaded directly by the camera. They want it done on-site. And then they still sometimes come out to spot check before they calibrate his headgate for water bounty.

But all their due diligence can't protect them from the likes of Lolo. Lolo has found the secret to eternal life as a tamarisk hunter. Unknown to the Interior Department and its BuRec subsidiary, he has been seeding new patches of tamarisk, encouraging vigorous brushy groves in previously cleared areas. He has hauled and planted healthy root balls up and down the river system in strategically hidden and inaccessible corridors, all in a bid for security against the swarms of other tamarisk hunters that scour these same tributaries. Lolo is crafty. Stands like this one, a quarter-mile long and thick with salt-laden tamarisk, are his insurance policy.

Documentation finished, he unstraps a folding saw, along with his rockbar and shovel, and sets his poison jugs on the dead salt bank. He starts cutting, slicing into the roots of the tamarisk, pausing every 30 seconds to spread Garlon 4 on the cuts, poisoning the tamarisk wounds faster than they can heal. But some of the best tamarisk, the most vigorous, he uproots and sets aside, for later use.

$2.88 a day, plus water bounty.

It takes Maggie's rolling bleating camel stride a week to make it back to Lolo's homestead. They follow the river, occasionally climbing above it onto cold mesas or wandering off into the open desert in a bid to avoid the skeleton sprawl of emptied towns. Guardie choppers buzz up and down the river like swarms of angry yellowjackets, hunting for porto-pumpers and wildcat diversions. They rush overhead in a wash of beaten air and gleaming National Guard logos. Lolo remembers a time when the guardies traded potshots with people down on the river banks, tracer-fire and machine-gun chatter echoing in the canyons. He remembers the glorious hiss and arc of a Stinger missile as it flashed across redrock desert and blue sky and burned a chopper where it hovered.

But that's long in the past. Now, guardie patrols skim up the river unmolested.

Lolo tops another mesa and stares down at the familiar landscape of an eviscerated town, its curving streets and subdivision cul-de-sacs all sitting silent in the sun. At the very edge of the empty town, one-acre ranchettes and snazzy five-thousand-square-foot houses with dead-stick trees and dust-hill landscaping fringe a brown tumbleweed golf course. The sandtraps don't even show any more.

When California put its first calls on the river, no one really worried. A couple of towns went begging for water. Some idiot newcomers with bad water rights stopped grazing their horses, and that was it. A few years later, people started showering real fast. And a few after that, they showered once a week. And then people started using the buckets. By then, everyone had stopped joking about how "hot" it was. It didn't really matter how "hot" it was. The problem wasn't lack of water or an excess of heat, not really. The problem was that 4.4 million acre-feet of water were supposed to go down the river to California. There was water; they just couldn't touch it.

They were supposed to stand there like dumb monkeys and watch it flow on by.

"Lolo?"

The voice catches him by surprise. Maggie startles and groans and lunges for the mesa edge before Lolo can rein her around. The camel's great padded feet scuffle dust and Lolo flails for his shotgun where it nestles in a scabbard at the camel's side. He forces Maggie to turn, shotgun half-drawn, holding barely to his seat and swearing.

A familiar face, tucked amongst juniper tangle.

"Goddamnit!" Lolo lets the shotgun drop back into its scabbard. "Jesus Christ, Travis. You scared the hell out of me."

Travis grins. He emerges from amongst the junipers' silver bark rags, one hand on his gray fedora, the other on the reins as he guides his mule out of the trees. "Surprised?"

"I could've shot you!"

"Don't be so jittery. There's no one out here 'cept us water ticks."

"That's what I thought the last time I went shopping down there. I had a whole set of new dishes for Annie and I broke them all when I ran into an ultralight parked right in the middle of the main drag."

"Meth flyers?"

"Beats the hell out of me. I didn't stick around to ask."

"Shit. I'll bet they were as surprised as you were."

"They almost killed me."

"I guess they didn't."

Lolo shakes his head and swears again, this time without anger. Despite the ambush, he's happy to run into Travis. It's lonely country, and Lolo's been out long enough to notice the silence of talking to Maggie. They trade ritual sips of water from their canteens and make camp together. They swap stories about BuRec and avoid discussing where they've been ripping tamarisk and enjoy the view of the empty town far below, with its serpentine streets and quiet houses and shining untouched river.

It isn't until the sun is setting and they've finished roasting a magpie that Lolo finally asks the question that's been on his mind ever since Travis's sun-baked face came out of the tangle. It goes against etiquette, but he can't help himself. He picks magpie out of his teeth and says, "I thought you were working downriver."

Travis glances sidelong at Lolo and in that one suspicious uncertain look, Lolo sees that Travis has hit a lean patch. He's not smart like Lolo. He hasn't been reseeding. He's got no insurance. He hasn't been thinking ahead about all the competition, and what the tamarisk endgame looks like, and now he's feeling the pinch. Lolo feels a twinge of pity. He likes Travis. A part of him wants to tell Travis the secret, but he stifles the urge. The stakes are too high. Water crimes are serious now, so serious Lolo hasn't even told his wife, Annie, for fear of what she'll say. Like all of the most shameful crimes, water theft is a private business, and at the scale Lolo works, forced labor on the Straw is the best punishment he can hope for.

Travis gets his hackles down over Lolo's invasion of his privacy and says, "I had a couple cows I was running up here, but I lost 'em. I think something got 'em."

"Long way to graze cows."

"Yeah, well, down my way even the sagebrush is dead. Big Daddy Drought's doing a real number on my patch." He pinches his lip, thoughtful. "Wish I could find those cows."

"They probably went down to the river."

Travis sighs. "Then the guardies probably got 'em."

"Probably shot 'em from a chopper and roasted 'em."

"Californians."

They both spit at the word. The sun continues to sink. Shadows fall across the town's silent structures. The rooftops gleam red, a ruby cluster decorating the blue river necklace.

"You think there's any stands worth pulling down there?" Travis asks.

"You can go down and look. But I think I got it all last year. And someone had already been through before me, so I doubt much is coming up."

"Shit. Well, maybe I'll go shopping. Might as well get something out of this trip."

"There sure isn't anyone to stop you."

As if to emphasize the fact, the thud-thwap of a guardie chopper breaks the evening silence. The black-fly dot of its movement barely shows against the darkening sky. Soon it's out of sight and cricket chirps swallow the last evidence of its passing.

Travis laughs. "Remember when the guardies said they'd keep out looters? I saw them on TV with all their choppers and Humvees and them all saying they were going to protect everything until the situation improved." He laughs again. "You remember that? All of them driving up and down the streets?"

"I remember."

"Sometimes I wonder if we shouldn't have fought them more."

"Annie was in Lake Havasu City when they fought there. You saw what happened." Lolo shivers. "Anyway, there's not much to fight for once they blow up your water treatment plant. If nothing's coming out of your faucet, you might as well move on."

"Yeah, well, sometimes I think you still got to fight. Even if it's just for pride." Travis gestures at the town below, a shadow movement. "I remember when all that land down there was selling like hotcakes and they were building shit as fast as they could ship in the lumber. Shopping malls and parking lots and subdivisions, anywhere they could scrape a flat spot."

"We weren't calling it Big Daddy Drought, back then."

"Forty-five thousand people. And none of us had a clue. And I was a real estate agent." Travis laughs, a self-mocking sound that ends quickly. It sounds too much like self-pity for Lolo's taste. They're quiet again, looking down at the town wreckage.

"I think I might be heading north," Travis says finally.

Lolo glances over, surprised. Again he has the urge to let Travis in on his secret, but he stifles it. "And do what?"

"Pick fruit, maybe. Maybe something else. Anyway, there's water up there."

Lolo points down at the river. "There's water."

"Not for us." Travis pauses. "I got to level with you, Lolo. I went down to the Straw."

For a second, Lolo is confused by the non sequitur. The statement is too outrageous. And yet Travis's face is serious. "The Straw? No kidding? All the way there?"

"All the way there." He shrugs defensively. "I wasn't finding any tamarisk, anyway. And it didn't actually take that long. It's a lot closer than it used to be. A week out to the train tracks, and then I hopped a coal train, and rode it right to the interstate, and then I hitched."

"What's it like out there?"

"Empty. A trucker told me that California and the Interior Department drew up all these plans to decide which cities they'd turn off when." He looks at Lolo significantly. "That was after Lake Havasu. They figured out they had to do it slow. They worked out some kind of formula: how many cities, how many people they could evaporate at a time without making too much unrest. Got advice from the Chinese, from when they were shutting down their old communist industries. Anyway, it looks like they're pretty much done with it. There's nothing moving out there except highway trucks and coal trains and a couple truck stops."

"And you saw the Straw?"

"Oh sure, I saw it. Out toward the border. Big old mother. So big you couldn't climb on top of it, flopped out on the desert like a damn silver snake. All the way to California." He spits reflexively. "They're spraying with concrete to keep water from seeping into the ground and they've got some kind of carbon-fiber stuff over the top to stop the evaporation. And the river just disappears inside. Nothing but an empty canyon below it. Bone-dry. And choppers and Humvees everywhere, like a damn hornet's nest. They wouldn't let me get any closer than a half mile on account of the eco-crazies trying to blow it up. They weren't nice about it, either."

"What did you expect?"

"I dunno. It sure depressed me, though: They work us out here and toss us a little water bounty and then all that water next year goes right down into that big old pipe. Some Californian's probably filling his swimming pool with last year's water bounty right now."

Cricket-song pulses in the darkness. Off in the distance, a pack of coyotes starts yipping. The two of them are quiet for a while. Finally, Lolo chucks his friend on the shoulder. "Hell, Travis, it's probably for the best. A desert's a stupid place to put a river, anyway."

Lolo's homestead runs across a couple acres of semi-alkaline soil, conveniently close to the river's edge. Annie is out in the field when he crests the low hills that overlook his patch. She waves, but keeps digging, planting for whatever water he can collect in bounty.

Lolo pauses, watching Annie work. Hot wind kicks up, carrying with it the scents of sage and clay. A dust devil swirls around Annie, whipping her bandana off her head. Lolo smiles as she snags it; she sees him still watching her and waves at him to quit loafing.

He grins to himself and starts Maggie down the hill, but he doesn't stop watching Annie work. He's grateful for her. Grateful that every time he comes back from tamarisk hunting she is still here. She's steady. Steadier than the people like Travis who give up when times get dry. Steadier than anyone Lolo knows, really. And if she has nightmares sometimes, and can't stand being in towns or crowds and wakes up in the middle of the night calling out for family she'll never see again, well, then it's all the more reason to seed more tamarisk and make sure they never get pushed off their patch like she was pushed.

Lolo gets Maggie to kneel down so he can dismount, then leads her over to a water trough, half-full of slime and water skippers. He gets a bucket and heads for the river while Maggie groans and complains behind him. The patch used to have a well and running water, but like everyone else, they lost their pumping rights and BuRec stuffed the well with Quickcrete when the water table dropped below the Minimum Allowable Reserve. Now he and Annie steal buckets from the river, or, when the Interior Department isn't watching, they jump up and down on a footpump and dump water into a hidden underground cistern he built when the Resource Conservation and Allowable Use Guidelines went into effect.

Annie calls the guidelines "RaCAUG" and it sounds like she's hawking spit when she says it, but even with their filled-in well, they're lucky. They aren't like Spanish Oaks or Antelope Valley or River Reaches: expensive places that had rotten water rights and turned to dust, money or no, when Vegas and L.A. put in their calls. And they didn't have to bail out of Phoenix Metro when the Central Arizona Project got turned off and then had its aqueducts blown to smithereens when Arizona wouldn't stop pumping out of Lake Mead.

Pouring water into Maggie's water trough, and looking around at his dusty patch with Annie out in the fields, Lolo reminds himself how lucky he is. He hasn't blown away. He and Annie are dug in. Calies may call them water ticks, but fuck them. If it weren't for people like him and Annie, they'd dry up and blow away the same as everyone else. And if Lolo moves a little bit of tamarisk around, well, the Calies deserve it, considering what they've done to everyone else.

Finished with Maggie, Lolo goes into the house and gets a drink of his own out of the filter urn. The water is cool in the shadows of the adobe house. Juniper beams hang low overhead. He sits down and connects his BuRec camera to the solar panel they've got scabbed onto the roof. Its charge light blinks amber. Lolo goes and gets some more water. He's used to being thirsty, but for some reason he can't get enough today. Big Daddy Drought's got his hands around Lolo's neck today.

Annie comes in, wiping her forehead with a tanned arm. "Don't drink too much water," she says. "I haven't been able to pump. Bunch of guardies around."

"What the hell are they doing around? We haven't even opened our headgates yet."

"They said they were looking for you."

Lolo almost drops his cup.

They know.

They know about his tamarisk reseeding. They know he's been splitting and planting root-clusters. That he's been dragging big healthy chunks of tamarisk up and down the river. A week ago he uploaded his claim on the canyon tamarisk—his biggest stand yet—almost worth an acre-foot in itself in water bounty. And now the guardies are knocking on his door.

Lolo forces his hand not to shake as he puts his cup down. "They say what they want?" He's surprised his voice doesn't crack.

"Just that they wanted to talk to you." She pauses. "They had one of those Humvees. With the guns."

Lolo closes his eyes. Forces himself to take a deep breath. "They've always got guns. It's probably nothing."

"It reminded me of Lake Havasu. When they cleared us out. When they shut down the water treatment plant and everyone tried to burn down the BLM office."

"It's probably nothing." Suddenly he's glad he never told her about his tamarisk hijinks. They can't punish her the same. How many acre-feet is he liable for? It must be hundreds. They'll want him, all right. Put him on a Straw work crew and make him work for life, repay his water debt forever. He's replanted hundreds, maybe thousands of tamarisk, shuffling them around like a cardsharp on a poker table, moving them from one bank to another, killing them again and again and again, and always happily sending in his "evidence."

"It's probably nothing," he says again.

"That's what people said in Havasu."

Lolo waves out at their newly tilled patch. The sun shines down hot and hard on the small plot. "We're not worth that kind of effort." He forces a grin. "It probably has to do with those enviro crazies who tried to blow up the Straw. Some of them supposedly ran this way. It's probably that."

Annie shakes her head, unconvinced. "I don't know. They could have asked me the same as you."

"Yeah, but I cover a lot of ground. See a lot of things. I'll bet that's why they want to talk to me. They're just looking for eco-freaks."

"Yeah, maybe you're right. It's probably that." She nods slowly, trying to make herself believe. "Those enviros, they don't make any sense at all. Not enough water for people, and they want to give the river to a bunch of fish and birds."

Lolo nods emphatically and grins wider. "Yeah. Stupid." But suddenly he views the eco-crazies with something approaching brotherly affection. The

Californians are after him, too.

Lolo doesn't sleep all night. His instincts tell him to run, but he doesn't have the heart to tell Annie, or to leave her. He goes out in the morning hunting tamarisk and fails at that as well. He doesn't cut a single stand all day. He considers shooting himself with his shotgun, but chickens out when he gets the barrels in his mouth. Better alive and on the run than dead. Finally, as he stares into the twin barrels, he knows that he has to tell Annie, tell her he's been a water thief for years and that he's got to run north. Maybe she'll come with him. Maybe she'll see reason. They'll run together. At least they have that. For sure, he's not going to let those bastards take him off to a labor camp for the rest of his life.

But the guardies are already waiting when Lolo gets back. They're squatting in the shade of their Humvee, talking. When Lolo comes over the crest of the hill, one of them taps the other and points. They both stand. Annie is out in the field again, turning over dirt, unaware of what's about to happen. Lolo reins in and studies the guardies. They lean against their Humvee and watch him back.

Suddenly Lolo sees his future. It plays out in his mind the way it does in a movie, as clear as the blue sky above. He puts his hand on his shotgun. Where it sits on Maggie's far side, the guardies can't see it. He keeps Maggie angled away from them and lets the camel start down the hill.

The guardies saunter toward him. They've got their

Humvee with a .50 caliber on the back and they've both got M-16s slung over their shoulders. They're in full bulletproof gear and they look flushed and hot. Lolo rides down slowly. He'll have to hit them both in the face. Sweat trickles between his shoulder blades. His hand is slick on the shotgun's stock.

The guardies are playing it cool. They've still got their rifles slung, and they let Lolo keep approaching. One of them has a wide smile. He's maybe 40 years old, and tanned. He's been out for a while, picking up a tan like that. The other raises a hand and says, "Hey there, Lolo."

Lolo's so surprised he takes his hand off his shotgun. "Hale?" He recognizes the guardie. He grew up with him. They played football together a million years ago, when football fields still had green grass and sprinklers sprayed their water straight into the air. Hale. Hale Perkins. Lolo scowls. He can't shoot Hale.

Hale says. "You're still out here, huh?"

"What the hell are you doing in that uniform? You with the Calies now?"

Hale grimaces and points to his uniform patches: Utah National Guard.

Lolo scowls. Utah National Guard. Colorado National Guard. Arizona National Guard. They're all the same. There's hardly a single member of the "National Guard" that isn't an out-of-state mercenary. Most of the local guardies quit a long time ago, sick to death of goose-stepping family and friends off their properties and sick to death of trading potshots with people who just wanted to stay in their homes. So even if there's still a Colorado National Guard, or an Arizona or a Utah, inside those uniforms with all their expensive nightsight gear and their brand-new choppers flying the river bends, it's pure California.

And then there are a few like Hale.

Lolo remembers Hale as being an OK guy. Remembers stealing a keg of beer from behind the Elks Club one night with him. Lolo eyes him. "How you liking that Supplementary Assistance Program?" He glances at the other guardie. "That working real well for you? The Calies a big help?"

Hale's eyes plead for understanding. "Come on, Lolo. I'm not like you. I got a family to look after. If I do another year of duty, they let Shannon and the kids base out of California."

"They give you a swimming pool in your backyard, too?"

"You know it's not like that. Water's scarce there, too."

Lolo wants to taunt him, but his heart isn't in it. A part of him wonders if Hale is just smart. At first, when California started winning its water lawsuits and shutting off cities, the displaced people just followed the water— right to California. It took a little while before the bureaucrats realized what was going on, but finally someone with a sharp pencil did the math and realized that taking in people along with their water didn't solve a water shortage. So the immigration fences went up.

But people like Hale can still get in.

"So what do you two want?" Inside, Lolo's wondering why they haven't already pulled him off Maggie and hauled him away, but he's willing to play this out.

The other guardie grins. "Maybe we're just out here seeing how the water ticks live."

Lolo eyes him. This one, he could shoot. He lets his hand fall to his shotgun again. "BuRec sets my headgate. No reason for you to be out here."

The Calie says, "There were some marks on it. Big ones."

Lolo smiles tightly. He knows which marks the Calie is talking about. He made them with five different wrenches when he tried to dismember the entire headgate apparatus in a fit of obsession. Finally he gave up trying to open the bolts and just beat on the thing, banging the steel of the gate, smashing at it, while on the other side he had plants withering. After that, he gave up and just carried buckets of water to his plants and left it at that. But the dents and nicks are still there, reminding him of a period of madness. "It still works, don't it?"

Hale holds up a hand to his partner, quieting him. "Yeah, it still works. That's not why we're here."

"So what do you two want? You didn't drive all the way out here with your machine gun just to talk about dents in my headgate."

Hale sighs, put-upon, trying to be reasonable. "You mind getting down off that damn camel so we can talk?"

Lolo studies the two guardies, figuring his chances on the ground. "Shit." He spits. "Yeah, OK. You got me." He urges Maggie to kneel and climbs off her hump. "Annie didn't know anything about this. Don't get her involved. It was all me."

Hale's brow wrinkles, puzzled. "What are you talking about?"

"You're not arresting me?"

The Calie with Hale laughs. "Why? Cause you take a couple buckets of water from the river? Cause you probably got an illegal cistern around here somewhere?" He laughs again. "You ticks are all the same. You think we don't know about all that crap?"

Hale scowls at the Calie, then turns back to Lolo. "No, we're not here to arrest you. You know about the Straw?"

"Yeah." Lolo says it slowly, but inside, he's grinning. A great weight is suddenly off him. They don't know. They don't know shit. It was a good plan when he started it, and it's a good plan still. Lolo schools his face to keep the glee off, and tries to listen to what Hale's saying, but he can't, he's jumping up and down and gibbering like a monkey. They don't know—

"Wait." Lolo holds up his hand. "What did you just say?"

Hale repeats himself. "California's ending the water bounty. They've got enough Straw sections built up now that they don't need the program. They've got half the river enclosed. They got an agreement from the Department of Interior to focus their budget on seep and evaporation control. That's where all the big benefits are. They're shutting down the water bounty payout program." He pauses. "I'm sorry, Lolo."

Lolo frowns. "But a tamarisk is still a tamarisk. Why should one of those damn plants get the water? If I knock out a tamarisk, even if Cali doesn't want the water, I could still take it. Lots of people could use the water."

Hale looks pityingly at Lolo. "We don't make the regulations, we just enforce them. I'm supposed to tell you that your headgate won't get opened next year. If you keep hunting tamarisk, it won't do any good." He looks around the patch, then shrugs. "Anyway, in another couple years they were going to pipe this whole stretch. There won't be any tamarisk at all after that."

"What am I supposed to do, then?"

"California and BuRec is offering early buyout money." Hale pulls a booklet out of his bulletproof vest and flips it open. "Sort of to soften the blow." The pages of the booklet flap in the hot breeze. Hale pins the pages with a thumb and pulls a pen out of another vest pocket. He marks something on the booklet, then tears off a perforated check. "It's not a bad deal."

Lolo takes the check. Stares at it. "Five hundred dollars?"

Hale shrugs sadly. "It's what they're offering. That's just the paper codes. You confirm it online. Use your BuRec camera phone, and they'll deposit it in whatever bank you want. Or they can hold it in trust until you get into a town and want to withdraw it. Any place with a BLM office, you can do that. But you need to confirm before April 15. Then BuRec'll send out a guy to shut down your headgate before this season gets going."

"Five hundred dollars?"

"It's enough to get you north. That's more than they're offering next year."

"But this is my patch."

"Not as long as we've got Big Daddy Drought. I'm sorry, Lolo."

"The drought could break any time. Why can't they give us a couple more years? It could break any time." But even as he says it, Lolo doesn't believe. Ten years ago, he might have. But not now. Big Daddy Drought's here to stay. He clutches the check and its keycodes to his chest.

A hundred yards away, the river flows on to California.

Paolo Bacigalupi is an internationally bestselling author of speculative fiction. He has won the Hugo, Nebula, World Fantasy, John W. Campbell and Locus Awards, as well as being a finalist for the National Book Award and a winner of the Michael L. Printz Award for Excellence in Young Adult Literature. Paolo's work often focuses on questions of sustainability and the environment, most notably the impacts of climate change. He has written novels for adults, young adults, and children, and is currently at work on a new novel. He can be found online at windupstories.com.

Our Sprinkler System

Lesley L. Smith

I smell smoke. I sniff deeply. Yep, that's smoke.

It reminds me of campfires with my husband David. Oh, my gosh. It reminds me of our honeymoon camping trip to Rocky Mountain National Park . . .

David lugged the cooler out of the back of the Subie (we called her Susie the Subie). "I can't believe you talked me into this, Lauren. Car camping isn't real camping. We should be hiking into the backcountry." He wore his favorite many-pocketed cargo shorts and his pink and blue plaid super-soft flannel shirt. When he wore that shirt, I'd sit next to him and stroke his arm.

I dumped the tent on a flat stretch of ground. "What can I say? I wanted lots of pillows and a comfy mattress for all our honeymoon-type activities. So sorry, not sorry."

When I glanced over at him at the picnic table, he grinned lasciviously. "You make a convincing argument, Wife."

"I know, Husband." I smiled back. "And you haven't even seen my sexy lingerie surprise for tonight."

He opened the cooler. "I brought you a surprise as well."

"You keep your sexy lingerie in the cooler? Interesting.

I did not know that." I chuckled as I walked over to him.

He pulled a red rose bud out of the cooler and handed it to me. "Ta-da."

"Very nice." I'd already deciphered he loved giving me flowers. And I loved receiving them. "Thanks." I sniffed. "It smells heavenly."

He pulled a bottle of champagne and two clear plastic flutes out of the ice-filled cooler.

"Even better," I said, grabbing one of the glasses. "Champagne me." I held the flute out as he removed the foil and little wire cage covering the cork. "Or should it be 'champers me'? Or maybe 'bubbly me'?"

His eyes sparkled. "Oh, don't worry, babe. I intend to champers you and bubbly you all night long."

Several hours later, we'd taken a break from honeymooning to build a fire and eat dinner. We each held a long stick with a marshmallow over the fire.

David's caught fire, and he pulled it toward him and blew it out, quickly shoving the molten sugar between two chocolate-encasing graham crackers. He held it out to me. "Here, babe."

"Thanks." I handed him my sugar-swabbed stick, and he handed me the treat. I took a big bite of melty-chocolatey-crunchy goodness. Mmm.

I sniff again. It smells just like that night. And what a great night it was. Even though it took place six decades ago, I still remember it like it was yesterday. It's funny how smells bring back memories.

Something beeps. What is that noise? It sort of sounds like my alarm clock.

I walk to the bedroom—so empty nowadays. Nope. No alarm clock going off. I'm tired; I sit for a few moments on the bed. Maybe I should take a nap? Somehow, I know David wouldn't want me to do that. He'd want me to find the sound. "Okay, babe." I force myself up off the bed.

I follow the noise out to the garage. It's coming from inside a cabinet. I pull open the door. Suddenly, the beeping is louder and insistent. It's blaring. A red light flashes. There's a little screen with red blinking letters. 'Fire Warning! Fire Warning!'

Oh, right. This is the fire suppression system David installed. When the fire department stopped covering our neighborhood, those of us left had to fend for ourselves.

It all started with a normal sprinkler system for our yard and extensive garden. But over the years, David expanded it until it was strong enough to protect the whole house from wildfire.

The beeping and flashing light are distracting. I can't concentrate. What am I supposed to do again? I wish David was here to help me. But he's not. He's been gone for a while.

How long has it been? I'm not sure . . . As I try to recall, I look at the apparatus.

Actually, knowing him, he would've left instructions somewhere around here.

Yes. That is just like him. He would've left instructions for me. I scrutinize the inside of the cabinet. Nothing. But, taped inside the cabinet door, I find a large sheet of paper with 'Instructions in case of a fire.'

"Yay, David." I read the instructions. They say how to turn off the alarms. I do so. The sudden quiet is lovely.

"What next, honey?"

'Check property perimeter. Ascertain fire location. If possible, flee the scene.'

"Makes sense, David, thanks." I march back into the house, over to the highest window, and examine the scene. In the distance, I see flames all the way around our house. They're not close, at least a block or two away, but they're there. "Shoot." I also notice there are no neighboring homes left.

When did that happen?

When David was in hospice in the family room, our nice next-door neighbor Mrs. Martinez brought him some of her world-famous flan. I asked her for the recipe. Did she ever give it to me? And another neighbor brought a big tray of tamales. Delicious. Who was that neighbor? David would know. Anyway, back then, we had some neighbors. Oh, right. The government tore down the houses after they moved away because of wildfire danger.

But I guess that was over two years ago . . . Yes. He's been gone for two-and-a-half years. Wow. It's hard to believe. How could I live two-and-a-half years without him? How could I live one minute without him?

How time flies. And at the same time, it drags. Each day seems to last forever, but all the days run together. It's hard to keep track of weeks, months, years . . .

Wait. What am I doing? I am doing something. Something for David. I am following his instructions.

Right. From the door in the cabinet in the garage.

I pace back to the garage.

'If you cannot flee, turn on the fire suppression system. Press the big green button.'

"Thanks, babe." I find the button and press it.

Nothing happens.

OUR SPRINKLER SYSTEM | 57

I go back inside the house and look out the window again. Clearly, nothing wet or sprinkly is happening. And the smoke scent is stronger now. Are the flames closer?

I rush to the garage to check the instructions.

'If the sprinkler doesn't come on, call for help.'

If only. I finger the phone in my pocket. Since we were unincorporated, emergency services won't come.

Lower on the sheet of instructions, it says, 'Annual Maintenance: Make sure to turn off and drain system in fall and turn on the system in spring.' Have I ever done that? I don't think so.

David handled all the household maintenance.

He passed in the winter, so maybe the system was still turned off for the winter?

I study the instruction sheet. 'Maintenance instructions: Get a flat screwdriver. Go outside to the left of the backdoor. Find the pipes for the sprinkler system. Align two screws vertically in the vertical pipe. Find the faucet head near the ground and turn it counterclockwise. Find the valve on the horizontal section and move parallel to the pipe. Listen for water flowing.'

Wow. That seems like a lot.

I don't think I can do it.

But if I don't do it . . .

The garage is getting smokier. Our home will burn. All our stuff will burn. The champagne bottle we saved from our honeymoon, the flowers he gave me that I dried and pressed. He gave me, and grew me, so many flowers over the years . . .

On our first date (about sixty years ago), he blindfolded me and held my hands as we strolled down the sidewalk.

"Uh, David," I said. "I don't mean to be a party pooper, but this is our first date; I'm not up for any weird S&M stuff." I snickered. I was joking because I didn't think he was into anything weird like bondage.

"Aw, Lauren," he said, taking off the blindfold. "Not even sunflowers and marigolds?"

I opened my eyes and saw a garden full of every color of the rainbow. "Where are we?" I recognized the sunflowers and marigolds, but there were dozens of blooms I didn't know. Wow.

"The Denver Botanic Gardens," he said, beaming and waving his hands around, gesturing at all the plants. "Have you been here before?"

"No." I shook my head. His enthusiasm was infectious. "I don't think so. I thought it would be boring, but it's beautiful."

"Close your eyes and smell the flowers." He closed his eyes and inhaled.

I closed my eyes and breathed deeply. Who knew flowers had so many different scents? Sweet. Spicy. Sour. All kinds of smells.

We spent hours strolling around, holding hands, looking at and smelling the flowers. And getting to know one another. I told him things I hadn't told anyone before.

As we sat on a bench surrounded by blooms, birds, and buzzing bees, his leg pressed against mine. "It's my dream to buy a home in the foothills and create a multicolored garden to share with . . . someone special."

I'd heard of someone walking over your grave, but that afternoon, I felt like someone was walking over my future. Despite the warming sun, I shivered in delight, or maybe anticipation.

To this day, the scent of flowers reminds me of David. But I'm not smelling flowers right now. I'm smelling . . . smoke.

Oh, right.

All the pictures of our life together might burn . . .

Me. I might burn up. My eyes start to water. It must be the smoke.

If I burn up, no one will remember our wonderful life together. No one will remember the camping, the honeymooning, the gardening and all the rest. No one will remember the average days: eating dinner and then sharing a coffee together on the back patio amidst the blooms as the sun sinks below the mountains. No one will remember us.

David wouldn't want that for me. He would want me to survive, to figure this out. That's why he left me instructions, right? I can picture him in his flannel shirt writing out all this stuff on this giant piece of paper and then, oh so carefully, taping it on the door.

He had faith in me, faith that I could figure it out. I would have to have faith in his faith.

I find a screwdriver in the toolbox.

I open the backdoor, and smoke wafts into the garage. "Shoot." I quickly shove the door closed.

I grab the N95 mask David left for me.

I brace myself and open the backdoor again and step outside.

Even through the mask, the smoke burns my throat.

I find the pipes to the left of the door. I align the screws. So far, so good.

But then, I have a heck of a time finding the faucet head.

I can't see because my eyes are watering. I start coughing. I drop the screwdriver.

I feel around in front of me. "Faucet. Where's the faucet?"

"You can do it, babe," David says.

I know the pipes are right in front of me. The faucet must be right in front of me, too. I scrabble around.

I find it. I turn it counterclockwise.

What was the last step?

"Shoot." I cough and cough. I can't remember the last step.

"Valve parallel," David says.

The valve. I felt it a moment ago on the pipe. I reach out and turn the valve. Creak.

Suddenly, there's a loud whooshing sound.

And then a loud spraying sound. Sshh. Drops of water caress my head and back.

And then I hear a sizzling sound. Ssss.

"It worked. It worked." I lean back. "Thank you, David." He said our sprinkler system was so big it could save the house.

I relax on the ground.

As the drops from the sprinkler system douse my face, they mingle with tears of relief.

And love.

"Thank you, Husband," I whisper.

"Thank you, Wife," he whispers back.

Lesley L. Smith, M.F.A, Ph.D., is a scientist and science fiction author. Her short stories have appeared in various venues including *Fiction River*, *Analog Science Fiction and*

Fact, and *Daily Science Fiction*. She has written several novels, including *The Quantum Cop, Conservation of Luck, Temporal Dreams*, and *Kat Cubed*. Check out her latest novel *A Discovery of Time and Space*, available where all fine books are sold! She's a longtime active member of RMFW and the Science Fiction/Fantasy Writers of America. Along with several other RMFW authors, she is a founder and editor of the ezine Electric Spec (electricspec.com). Send Electric Spec your stories. For more info, check out Lesley's online home at lesleylsmith.com.

Rightsizing

Jeff Jaskot

Alejandra stabbed at the radio's presets, in search of a decent tune to keep her company. Giving up, she squealed her tires turning onto Highway 59 just as a prairie dog scampered across. She aimed, swerved, but missed the critter. The little bastard reared up in her rearview mirror, threw its head back, and screeched the equivalent of "bitch" her way.

"Nothing personal," said Alejandra. The rodent shrank in her mirror. "Just you or us. That's all."

Probably a good thing she hadn't killed it. If tagged, the Eco-Balance team would have investigated. If found intentional, she'd be out of her water enforcement job.

Then again, would that be all bad?

For two decades, straight out of UNC, Alejandra had been the water conservation officer over the Yuma Water Co-op. Once a job that held some power and latitude, now she was little more than a monitor. Tagging and tracking anything that could slurp water: human, bovine, bird, reptile, or rodent. Ensuring the irrigation systems worked properly. Checking the levels of the aquifer, the security of hardened wells, and the soundness of the storage tanks. She had done well and risen to senior officer, but that only meant she got all the dirty jobs.

So when Ray Jevons, the first water right owner of the Yuma Co-op, had called an hour ago with an urgent summons requesting her, she had to oblige. So said the archaic laws. She shouldn't complain. It had been nearly a year since her last visit there, a record for Ray.

With the sun setting, Alejandra turned into Jevons's dusty quarter-mile driveway. The cows were out and trying to reach the wheatgrass down in the ditches. This early in the season, everything else still slumbered brown. The sensors on her truck ticked as they counted numbers, sizes, and sexes of the tagged livestock in range. No alarms thankfully; nothing untagged.

She reached the old farmhouse—humble for such a large spread—and parked. A light burned upstairs. Stepping onto the wooden front porch, she rapped on the screen door and braced herself.

Ray's distant voice cut through the thin walls and peeling paint. "Come 'round back!"

Alejandra sighed and made her way around the wraparound porch. A stench from the east wafted from the cattle pens. Near the back door, she noticed he'd planted hydrangea bushes again. Non-native, exceptionally thirsty, toxic to humans and wildlife, she'd have to report it. But not tonight.

Tonight, you listen, nod, and get the hell home.

She cupped her hands on the screen door and peered in. "Hey, Ray. You called?"

"Come on in, Allie." Ray stood at the kitchen sink, doing dishes by hand. His tall, thin frame stooped precariously over the marred countertop.

Alejandra entered but stayed near the screen door. The grassy, greasy odor of Ray and his wife, both in their nineties, permeated the couple's home. But it was the acrid recycled dishwater that pushed her nose to the brink. Blinking red lights flashed on the recycler under the sink, likely months of meals caked the filters.

The RF detector above her chattered, unsure if she was in or out.

Taking a deep breath, she stepped in further and waved her hand high until it stopped. The lights on the RF detector had been taped over.

"You know that tape doesn't do anything," said Alejandra.

With a face as pruned as his dishpan hands, Ray glanced at her then the detector. "I know that. I once ran this co-op. Just can't stand Big Bother winking at me all the time."

"It just tracks types of tags and keeps a count. Not your every move."

Ray huffed and finished the dishes.

"Will Lily be joining us?"

"No. She's been bedridden for a couple months now. Another round of skin cancer."

"Oh, sorry to hear that," said Alejandra. She liked Lily, a wise woman, always pleasant, kind-hearted, often willing to help chip away at her husband.

Ray wiped his hands, tossed the towel in the sink, and got to his agenda. "My granddaughter wants to have a baby."

Alejandra winced. "Maddie's not pregnant, is she?" The poor girl had already suffered through two abortions.

Ray looked Alejandra straight on. "No, she's not pregnant." He fished the dish towel out of the sink and folded it. "She's just off visiting her in-laws in Grand Junction. I plan to have good news for her when she gets back."

Had Ray ever bothered to read the co-op's newsletters? For over two years now, it clearly stated, "Due to strict quotas, pregnancy requests are not being considered at this time." And even if they were, Maddie would have to add her name to a long waitlist.

"I'm sorry, Ray. There are no more human RFIDs for our co-op. There's nothing I can do."

He leaned toward her. "I don't believe that. We had a good precip year. Best in decades."

"We sure did. Now we need about a thousand more years just like it. We're doing OK up top. But the aquifer is as low as it's ever been. We're still pumping too much water."

Ray held out a trembling finger. "There's no way to know that for sure."

"Technology has changed, Ray. We've got probes all throughout the Ogallala Aquifer now. I've seen the data."

"But I'm talking human lives. Doesn't that mean anything anymore?"

"To me, yes," she said, raising her voice for the first time, having known the unexpected pain of a mandatory abortion. "But AI sets the quotas nowadays. And the water courts aren't budging on any exceptions to the recommendations. Not even for human populations."

"Populations, models, projections. Just made-up numbers." Still holding the folded towel, the old man backed off, groaned down into a kitchen chair, and motioned for Alejandra to sit in the other. "Look, I'm willing to give up whatever it takes. A hundred head, a thousand acres. Name your price."

Alejandra sat across from him. "Doesn't work that way anymore, Ray. Nothing sucks up water like adding more people. And subtracting crops and livestock just compounds the balance problem. People start to starve. You know we're farming more desert than plains now. And the only way to turn that around is to maintain a strict balance between us, nature, and the aquifer." Out of habit, she blurted the water officer's motto as if she were presenting to a third-grade classroom. "Sip today to blossom tomorrow."

A mournful cry from upstairs paused their conversation.

Alejandra trembled as it peaked then faded. "Is that Lily?"

Ray waved it off. "About time for her pain meds. Let's settle this first."

Still rattled, Alejandra thought to argue. Lily sounded like she needed her meds. But Alejandra knew Ray. They would have to finish their business before his wife would get relief.

Alejandra offered an option. "Look, your granddaughter and her husband can move. The Great Lakes are welcoming everyone, looking to grow their population. I can arrange that."

He twisted the towel in his hands and shook his head.

"I could even arrange for you and your whole family to move."

Salt, pepper, and hot sauce shakers tumbled when Ray's palm smacked the table. "You'd like that. Kick me off my family's land. Get rid of me and my first water rights for good. The Jevons have been here for over 150 years. We're not budging."

Upstairs, Lily once more wailed for her husband. This time she droned on.

Tired, uneasy, agitated, Alejandra put it blankly. "Ray, you and your water rights are pretty much ceremonial now."

She started righting the shakers. "I'm just doing my job. And if I do it well, the aquifer quits dropping. If the next generation comes along and does their jobs, the levels may start to rise. And maybe fifty generations from now, after you and I are long gone, that aquifer is healthy again. Until then, there's no talking about individual water rights."

Alejandra sat back in her chair and prepared for the explosion, but it never came. Instead, Ray closed his eyes and let his head tip back.

"Ray?"

Lily let out a scream of agony. Ray stayed motionless. Alejandra rose, debating whether to flat-out leave or rush upstairs.

"Can you stay until I get Lily settled down?" Ray opened his eyes and made his way to a tray of meds. "I need you to take care of one more thing for me, Allie."

"Well, I . . ."

"Just be a minute." He started up the creaky stairs. Lily whimpered at his approach. "Maybe two."

Alejandra sat for two, then five minutes. She got up to pace around the kitchen, noting the dead houseplants, the countertop filled with prescriptions, a refrigerator that smelled worse than the overflowing garbage can. She would reach out to elder services tomorrow, whether Ray approved or not.

Stepping into the front room, Alejandra admired the mishmash of standalone bookshelves lining the walls, stuffed with actual hold-in-your-hand paper books. Under lamps and near windows, empty teacups and half-spent scented candles littered Lily's informal library.

Alejandra recognized a few titles from her only long-ago English Lit class: *A Tale of Two Cities*, *Fahrenheit 451*, *To*

Kill a Mockingbird. She owned e-glasses but never seemed to find the time to read anything beyond mail, work-related docs, and ecological articles. Too often, she spent her nights flittering about the metaverse, downing a couple of bulldogs along the way, heavy on the cream, light on the fizz.

Inspired by warm memories of Lily, her collection, wit, and endless cheerfulness, Alejandra would download a book when she got home. Maybe even start to read it tonight. With a cup of tea, no cream, no fizz.

Another cry stopped Alejandra's exploration, this time different in tone and location. Alejandra moved to a faded pink door under the stairs and placed an ear against a wood panel. For several breaths she only heard her heartbeat, and then it sounded again. Not an old woman's moan of pain, but a faint, needy cry.

When she turned the knob, the door creaked open, revealing dark steps leading down. Alejandra searched for a light switch, but there was none. She descended, her body casting a long shadow.

Halfway down, her eyes adjusted enough to make out a landing at the bottom with a closed door on the left. Yellow light seeped out from underneath. She stopped when shadows raced across.

Heart pounding, Alejandra decided to retreat. But as she turned to climb, a blinding light tripped her up. Stumbling, shading her eyes, she clung to the railing.

"See you found your way," said Ray, releasing the pull chain of the bare lightbulb above his head. He stood at the top of the stairwell, blocking the way.

"What? I just . . ."

Motioning with something in his hand, Ray said, "Doesn't matter anymore. Go on down. Go on in."

Shaking, Alejandra knew she could likely power her way up—depending on what the old man held in his hand. But the beseeching cry rang out again, this time clear. Another voice joined in, even louder. The sounds were unmistakable and unbelievable.

Alejandra steadied herself with the railing and started down. Reaching the bottom, she took a deep breath and threw open the door without entering. Smells of damp diapers and disinfectant washed over her.

Maddie stood inside holding a baby no more than a month old. Her husband, Chayton, cradled another as he sat and swung in a gliding rocker. Both babies dressed warmly in orange and navy-blue caps and onesies, Alejandra assumed twin boys.

"Hello, Alejandra," said a pale but smiling Maddie. "You're their first visitor. This is Calder and that's Tahoe."

Stepping in, Alejandra noticed a wall of boxed baby supplies: formula, diapers, and wipes. Diaper pails and hampers sat by portable cribs. Neatly folded clean clothes, infant and adult, sat stacked on separate racks by a washer and dryer. A fridge, freezer, hot plate, and microwave lined the far wall.

"Maddie, what have you done?"

"What we had to do," said Maddie, showing Calder to Alejandra. "Once I knew I was pregnant, I hid it for as long as I could before disappearing down here. Not a bad nest, considering."

"Ray said you were visiting relatives in the mountains." Alejandra looked at the baby's palm. "He's untagged."

"Of course, that's the whole point of this," said Ray, standing in the doorway.

Alejandra spun to face him.

He held out a plastic baggie with a poorly bandaged hand. Blood dripped down his palm onto the plastic, concealing its contents.

"Take it," commanded Ray.

Alejandra stared at the crimson-smeared bag. "Shit, Ray. You shouldn't have done that." She pinched the only clean corner, taking it from him, turning it to verify. "Without your RFIDs, you and Lily can't even leave this house now."

"I know. I helped write that rule. 'Removal of tags is punishable by immediate expulsion from the co-op,'" he said.

"They'll take you away. You can never come back," Alejandra pointed out. "Is Lily on board with this?"

Ray chuckled. "This was all her idea."

"Can I talk to her?" asked Alejandra, setting the baggie on a changing table, fearing the worst.

Looking down, Ray clamped his craggy mouth and shook his head. Maddie began to cry. Chayton's rocking quickened.

What did you do, you stubborn old fool? Alejandra raked her face then dragged a hand through her hair. *What should I do?*

"It's not that simple, Ray. You can't just bequeath tags. Given the latest numbers, we're not at our quota, we're over! They won't reallocate these tags."

"Lily thought of that," he said, unconcerned. "That's why she had me call you."

"Me? I don't tag humans. They do that at hospitals."

"What's a human but an animal that overthinks things."

"This ain't right, Ray."

"Look, Allie, only the adults in this room will ever know the truth. You said yourself that Big Bother only tracks numbers, not specifics. We do this right, and nobody will ever find out." Ray motioned to Maddie. "Before you decide . . ."

The young mother stepped up, gave Calder a kiss on his cap, and placed the infant in the water officer's arms.

Chayton rose. Tahoe floated in the big man's embrace until eased into Alejandra's open arm.

Alejandra watched the two brothers coo and kick at one another as she considered her options. She could turn them down and get the whole family thrown out of the water co-op—if they let her leave. She could do as they asked and afterwards, when safe, reveal the plot. There certainly would be a story to tell, maybe even a promotion. Or she could play along, break her oath, and help cultivate a new generation of High Plains agrarians.

Done squirming, the boys drifted off to sleep in Alejandra's arms. She sighed at the sight and gave her answer. "I'll need my kit."

Maddie hugged her. Ray slapped her on the back and then took Chayton aside.

Alejandra gingerly gave the twins back to their mother before stepping between the men. There was one last qualm to shake. "You sure about this, Ray? You're the one giving up everything."

The old man seemed confused. "Lily is already gone. Nothing left but to join her."

For the first time, Alejandra saw the fight go out of Ray's eyes. He suddenly seemed his age.

"All right." Alejandra committed. "For this to work, it needs to look like an accident. Something capable of destroying RFID tags."

"Chayton and I got that all worked out. You just get my

great-grandkids tagged."

Alejandra left the basement, exiting the back door to a click of the RF scanner. Grabbing a long-handled shovel left by the newly planted hydrangeas, she stepped back and opened the screen door, careful not to enter. With a couple of underhanded swings, she smashed the scanner. It dangled briefly from Ray's black tape before crashing onto the kitchen floor. With satisfaction, she flattened it with a final two-handed whack.

As far as Big Bother was concerned, only one person had left the Jevonses' place. A "down scanner" alarm would get reported, but it was after hours. No tech would bother to check on it until morning.

Still, they moved quickly.

Chayton, under Ray's direction, loaded up his truck with all the baby gear and supplies, right down to the full diaper pails.

As Maddie brought the babies out of the basement and out into their new world, Alejandra washed clean the bloody RFID tags in alcohol. The microchips were old but still a supported model. Using a prairie dog syringe, she injected a tag into a sleeping Tahoe's tiny palm and then one into a fussy Calder. Neither cried, which Alejandra took as a good sign.

Packing up her gear, Alejandra gave instructions to Maddie. "If anyone asks about the tags, Maddie, just send them my way. Us bureaucrats are fucking things up all the time. I can cover until people move on. For tonight, go stay at the old Riley place. It's been decommissioned for a few years now."

Maddie's eyes went wide. "How long do we have to stay there?"

"No need to hunker down. After tonight, you'll have the perfect reason to come home. Figure a day or two to get word, pack up, and make your way 'back' from Grand Junction. People will be gossiping so much about what happened to your grandparents that a couple of newborn twins will just be a side story." Alejandra looked at the peaceful faces of the slumbering babies. "In fact, be sure to show them off. Nothing's more comforting than new life arriving on the heels of death."

"Allie? You ready?" Ray shuffled up, followed by Chayton, who hoisted the two dismantled cribs into the truck bed.

She nodded. "The boys are tagged. I manually scanned them just to make sure the tags work. You're all set. I'm all set."

Preparations done, Alejandra stood there. A sudden wave of dread filled her. She could see the same in Maddie and Chayton's faces as well. Ray straightened, looking twenty years younger, to show he was ready.

"I'll just check inside one last time," Alejandra lied, letting the family share a final moment, trying to hold it together herself.

Inside, she saw that Ray had put together another tray of meds, this time for himself. She moved into the front room/library. As she ran her hand along the bookshelves, she stopped at one book that spoke to her.

"Find something you like?" It was Ray, alone and still standing tall. "Take whatever you like. Lily said I should thank you somehow."

Alejandra took the well-worn book from its perch. "*The Good Earth*."

"Lily liked that one. She read it a few times. Never read

much myself, but that's one I might've thumbed through."

Ray turned back into the kitchen and grabbed the tray. "See yourself out, Allie." He went up one step, then another.

Alejandra—clutching her book, head down, eyes tearing—started for the back door.

Ray stopped halfway up. "Allie, you did the right thing. Remember that."

She stayed until he disappeared up the stairs, his footsteps creaking across floorboards. Then she joined the young family outside.

Chayton waited a few minutes, comforting Maddie and the babies, who were up again. Taking a deep breath, he headed into the house on shaky legs.

Alejandra couldn't see much, just shadows. She took the time to wish Maddie luck and marvel one more time at the baby blue eyes of the brothers. Getting into her truck, she smelled smoke and saw Chayton dashing out the back door.

The light upstairs was still on as she drove down the driveway. The front room below glowed orange.

A mile down the road, from her rearview mirror, Ray and Lily's house lit up the prairie. Yuma Fire and Rescue would be on the way soon, so she turned off the highway and onto the dirt roads.

Being the last known person to visit the Jevons, she practiced her half-truth.

Ray wanted to talk about his water rights. He felt they weren't being honored. I told him the current state of the aquifer. He slammed the table and cussed at me, our technology, the co-op, the water courts. Lily started screaming in pain upstairs. She had cancer, I think. He had to go to her, so he told me to "Go on. Get out." I left him in a shitty mood.

I listened. I nodded. I honored his rights.
It stank.

After multiple degrees in computer science and a successful career in the health care industry, **Jeff Jaskot** recently moved with his wife from metro Detroit to Northern Colorado. He now enjoys ample time to write science fiction (concentrating on climate fiction) and mysteries. He was a short story winner (mystery) and runner-up (sci-fi) in back-to-back issues of *On the Premises* magazine.

Attack of the Third Planet

Collin Irish

On September 15, 2017, the Cassini spacecraft descended into the atmosphere of Saturn and broke apart in the delicate ecosystem of the Kytimmer. The subsequent environmental collapse resulted in millions of deaths and rendered the planet unable to support life. The survivors traced the path of the doomsday device to its origin. On the third planet orbiting the sun, they found a potential new home and a chance for justice.

A latex-wrapped tentacle reached through the isolation pod portal, and Lexi cuddled it against her face and neck. She hugged her mother in the only way possible since Lexi became human.

"Lexi." The monotone voice emitted from a speaker mounted just above the portal. It vibrated the air in her bubble so Lexi's alien ears could hear her mother's words. "You look nice this morning."

"Thanks, Mom." Lexi moved her mouth and tongue as she'd been taught. They were much more complicated communication mechanisms than the usual vibration membranes of her species. It had taken all six Earth years since her transformation to master the sound manipulation using variations in air pressure. "I'm trying a new style."

Lexi brushed the long strands of straight black hair away from one side of her forehead, leaving the other side of her face covered and revealing only one of her dark brown eyes.

Her mother's single eye peered through the chamber's observation port, almost bumping into it. The eye rippled through a spectrum of color variations as her mother focused. She stopped on a bright green with yellow stripes and a deep black aperture. "Is this a typical human hair style?"

Lexi frowned as the speaker crackled, missing a couple of subtle Kytimmer intonations. She filled in enough to understand her mother's words.

"There are some like it from Earth's video feeds. I think it looks good on me."

"You look beautiful."

Lexi rolled her eyes but smiled anyway. She had no idea how her human looks would compare to the real thing. Kytimmer scientists, like her mother, had worked tirelessly to advance genetic engineering and transform her. No one knew how well the disguise would work.

The isolation pod rocked as Lexi's mother wrapped her remaining seven tentacles around its translucent walls. Green suction cups with deep blue veins gripped the pod. Her mother's scaly gray-and-black flesh pressed against the pressurized chamber, and she squeezed. Lexi's little air bubble flexed, and the surrounding hydrogen and helium gas swirled with turbulence.

Lexi frowned and crossed her arms. Her mother always found an excuse to be dramatic. "Easy, Mom. Don't burst my bubble."

"I just want to hug you properly. I haven't had the chance in a long time." Her mother eased off the embrace. "You're doing so well. Your father would have been proud."

Lexi's heart fluttered in her chest and tears welled in her eyes—reactions perfectly designed to emulate human emotional responses. Lexi supposed loss and grief hurt just as much for humans as her own kind. Being neither, however, meant she had to trust science for accuracy.

Her mother lifted Lexi's isolation chamber onto her muscular back and set off through the ship. She half-crawled, half-floated in the low gravity, maintained at Earth standard for Lexi's benefit. Bladders along her sides ejected jets of gas to keep her aloft while crossing the interior's cavernous expanse.

Lexi crossed her arms and plopped into the seat at the control console. "You don't have to carry me, Mom. I can fly my pod."

"Nonsense. I hardly see you these days with all the drop preparations." Her mother's voice rumbled with emotional turmoil, and the speaker managed to translate enough for Lexi to hear the sadness barely veiled by forced cheer.

Lexi pouted, but she couldn't deny her mother's attachment, nor did she want to. The other children didn't have a doting parent. An abundance of orphans was one of the consequences of war. Still, she'd rather fly the pod and dock it into her deployment station on her own like everyone else.

"Here we are." Her mom lifted Lexi off her back and onto the platform overlooking the deployment station hub. An array of spherical bowls encircled a central set of screens. Data of all sorts flashed across the screens in front of already occupied stations. A single inhabitant, much like Lexi, lived in each pod.

"Bye, Mom." Lexi took the controls and flitted with easy

grace through the swirling gases to settle into her workstation. The screens lit up as her external data port linked with the system.

"Welcome, Cadet Lexi." The AI's voice came through her speaker without distortion. Tons of research on human speech patterns went into the design of its insipidly cheerful tone.

"Thank you, Hub." Lexi checked her rear-view monitor. Her mother lingered on the balcony above like she always did. Lexi pretended not to notice like she always did.

"Today's mission briefing and task descriptions have been downloaded into your personal files. Please proceed with the training protocols when ready."

"Acknowledged." Lexi pressed the correct sequence of keys to display the day's lesson files. An impossible task for her kind. With the addition of bones into her anatomy, she did the impossible every day. Pushing buttons on a keyboard, walking on two legs in a delicate balance of coordination and timing, folding joints at right angles, controlling a bobbling head. Miracles or oddities, depending on the beholder. Standing out in either way stirred her anxiety, but she tamped down the feeling.

"Lexi!" Daniel shouted into his intercom as usual. Digitally generated explosions resounded in the background. "I'm gonna beat your score on Attack of the Third Planet."

Lexi thumbed her intercom open. "You'll never do it. You might destroy more invading ships, but you have to fight the resulting environmental disaster too. Takes more than big guns."

"That part doesn't count."

"It counts, Daniel." Anna joined the conference line.

"It's half the score. You'll never beat Lexi. She saved Kytim. Or at least the simulated version of it."

"Geek! Only the combat score really counts." Devastating explosions emanated from Daniel's pod. "Oh, dang!" His game ended.

Lexi turned the volume down on his cursing and smiled at Anna. "Thanks."

Anna grinned back. "He's dreaming if he thinks he can beat your score."

Lexi managed to beat the game one time, but even that victory cost too many simulated lives. Winning didn't make her feel any better about their actual losses from the human invasion. Her father being one of them. She stopped that line of thought before it could take hold.

"What's new on the chatter-board?" Lexi asked. The com data emanating from Earth never ceased. Nor did the ignorant Earthlings take measures to secure it, broadcasting free intelligence into space. The Kytimmer armada didn't need spies, at least not yet.

"Same old stuff." Anna pressed a button on her console, and data streamed across her display. "No sign of detection. Our dark matter shield must be doing the trick. I wonder how close we can get?"

"Probably as close as their moon. Any closer and the swarm of attack ships orbiting their planet will perturbate and give us away." Lexi smiled with confidence in her astrophysics skills.

"The humans say those are weather satellites and other observational devices, not attack ships." Anna's mouth drew into a skeptical frown.

"Sure they are." The humans even claimed the doomsday ship that destroyed Kytim's livable climate was

ATTACK OF THE THIRD PLANET | 81

solely scientific. Whether this was a lie or a vast level of incompetence, they had to be brought to justice.

"Hello, Cadets." Hub's voice interrupted their conference line. "Congratulations on reaching a new phase of your training."

"Oh yeah!" Daniel pumped his fist. Anna leaned toward her screen, focusing all her attention. Lexi raised her eyebrows in an imitation of human surprise. She hadn't expected to transition to the next segment this soon.

"Moving from generic training to specialized skill enhancement will be challenging, but the operations staff will support you all the way." A spotlight lit the row of balcony workstations surrounding the hub. A few of the Kytimmer engineers waved a tentacle, but most kept working. Lexi's mother didn't serve in mission operations, so Lexi didn't look for her.

"Your Earth drop assignments are ready for review." Lexi's on-board server chimed at the arrival of a new encrypted file. "Please study your assignments carefully. Specialized skill training will begin after the ten minutes allotted for familiarization."

Lexi converted the Earth time to the Kytim clock to figure out how long she had to study. She and all her fellow cadets lived by the Earth clock, which was hard to get used to. Earth days lasted too long, but Earth years flitted by so quickly they were hard to grasp.

"JPL better watch out!" Daniel's enthusiasm crackled over the speaker. "Gonna blast the place." He made sounds from the video game with his mouth while pointing a finger in the air. Odd behaviors, but entirely accurate according to their briefing on human culture.

"What's JPL?" Anna asked.

"A place that's going down," Daniel shouted as he stomped around his bubble shooting imaginary enemies.

Lexi ignored him as she scanned her file. It had a collection of common mission data shared with her teammates. "Jet Propulsion Lab. An installation on the western coast of the northern continent. Housed many builders of the doomsday device."

"We're not supposed to blow them up, are we?" Anna leaned even closer to her bubble screen, and her face zoomed in on Lexi's display. Her furrowed brow and slight bite of the lip made for a perfect depiction of human nerves. Nice work. Lexi hoped her own imitation of anxiety would be just as convincing. It sure felt real.

"No, only reconnaissance at first. Our mission parameters are very strict. Only the Council of Elders can issue punishment for crimes against Kytim." Lexi tried to sound confident for Anna. The truth, however, included the possibility of violence during their infiltration phase. "Daniel is just having his fun. Where are you going?"

"Says here, Cape Canaveral. Same continent but opposite coast. I hope it's nice."

Lexi shrugged, not knowing how to define *nice* when combining an alien body with an alien planet. She scrolled to Anna's section of the mission briefing. "Cape Canaveral is the launch complex used to send the doomsday device to our planet. Many guilty humans live there."

"Could take some time to find them all." Anna bit her lip again. "What about you?"

Lexi brought up her own section. "A research and manufacturing installation in a place called Colorado near a city called Denver. It lies between your and Daniel's assignments on the same continent. There must be a lot of guilty people clumped together on that small stretch of land."

The thought of land brought a shiver of anxiety. Why would any species live on solid ground when they could float in the clouds? The bones in her body made such an arrangement possible, but it felt wrong.

"Aren't they all guilty?" Anna leaned back from the screen and looked at Lexi directly through the transparent walls of their bubbles. "I mean they almost wiped us out, Lexi. The most populous layers of Kytim were instantly rendered deathly toxic—a cascading environmental disaster. Millions upon millions died. How could they not all be guilty?"

Lexi wondered at the ability of such a small planet to cause so much trouble. She shrugged. "Maybe they are. We don't know. We're not like them. We don't carelessly or indiscriminately take life like they did. We have morals, standards, and values. You know all this, Anna." Lexi moved to the side of her bubble nearest Anna's and spread her arms wide, placing her palms on the transparent wall. Anna matched her, and they stared at each other with alien eyes into alien faces.

She wished for the thousandth time she could step outside of her confined space. She wished she could float away among the swirling clouds of the ship with her friends like a proper Kytimmer. Better yet, fly through the vast layers of Kytim like she did as a larva. Only brief impressions of her childhood remained. The strobing lights of storms. Colorful ammonia crystals. Rings of ice arcing across the sky. Her mother's musical laughter. Her father's embrace.

Lexi let the memories recede. She couldn't leave her

bubble, at least not here, and no one could go back to Kytim.

"I'm scared," Anna said in a small voice that barely registered on the com system.

Lexi nodded. "Me too. It's okay to be scared. I think everyone is. Even Daniel."

Tears welled up in Anna's hazel eyes. One slowly spilled over onto her cheek and glimmered. A rendition of human vulnerability so beautiful Lexi felt her own tears forming.

"We're going to get this mission done. Do our part to exact justice. We'll work together the whole time. You, me, and even Daniel."

Anna wiped her face. "Okay. I think I can do it. It's hard, but I can do it."

"Yes, you can. We all can." Lexi sounded more confident than she felt. Still, reassuring a friend felt good. It helped with her own fears too. Was this accurate human behavior? Whether or not it fit the mission profile, Lexi decided to keep empathizing with her friends.

A chime from Hub brought their attention back to their screens. "Attention Cadets. New information is available to share for your after-mission roles."

Lexi returned to her console and sat back into the chair. She felt the odd comfort of its pressure against her body. No such equivalent furniture existed for the Kytimmer. Having a skeleton brought with it many differences.

"After the first phase of your mission is complete and you have identified all culpable humans in your assigned location, you will proceed to a safe zone." Maps unfurled on Lexi's screen. An indicator marked an isolated place not far from her target industrial complex. "A pressurized living space much like your current bubble will be waiting. Once everyone is safe, we'll begin the second phase of the mission."

"Is that when we blast 'em?" Daniel jumped from his seat, ready to charge into battle.

"No, Cadet Daniel. That is when we deploy a series of atmospheric catalysts and transform the upper layers of Earth's atmosphere into a proper mixture of hydrogen and helium designed to stabilize into a livable region. Only a thin layer of nitrogen and oxygen will remain near the Earth's surface. Enough to keep most humans alive but not conscious."

"Seems a bit too easy to blast them at that point." Daniel's energy flagged. There would be no pitched battle against their foes. Lexi noticed Anna relax as well. An easier ending than she had imagined.

"No blasting will be necessary," Hub said. "Once the humans are subdued, we'll sort out the guilty, send them to the Kytim tribunal, and allow the rest to live in designated areas on the land. The rest of the planet will be transformed into our new home."

"No revenge?" Daniel pouted as he sat. "I was looking forward to exploring the human modes of vengeance and retribution."

"I'm sorry, Daniel," Hub said, "but I don't believe you will need to. Any other questions?"

Lexi keyed her microphone. "Yeah. What happens then?"

"The tribunal will determine justice and carry it out as mercifully as possible. We're not barbarians."

"No, I mean after that." Apprehension tickled her human guts. Though a very accurate sensation, pride did not accompany it. "Will we have to remain human?" As the question left her throat, she realized she had never thought beyond her mission. Would she forever be traveling about in this ridiculous shell of a body? In this lonely bubble? Surely the transformation could be reversed.

"Scientists are developing ways to address your genetic modifications. Until then, you will have choices for where you can live in your bubble. Back on the ship. In the atmosphere. In the transformed seas. Traveling back and forth as you please."

Hub paused, and when Lexi didn't speak, Hub continued answering questions from the other cadets. Lexi muted the speaker.

Lexi's mom was one of those scientists. If there were a way for Lexi to live a normal life, her mother would know about it. Icy fear stabbed her in the stomach. Her mother hadn't found a way. The realization struck hard. It couldn't be done. She would never be properly hugged by her own kind. By building her this way, her people had trapped her forever in the tiny world of one bubble.

Lexi's guts twisted, and she gasped for breath to keep up with her pounding heart. She fumbled for the pod controls and broke loose from the deployment station.

"Cadet Lexi, you haven't been dismissed," Hub called over her speaker.

Lexi turned off Hub's feed as she jerked the pod onto a course, any course, away from the drop station.

Lexi barged through the threshold of her mother's lab. She stood in the middle of her pod, itching to release all her emotions in a single burst. Work benches held a variety of tools of the trade. Vials of liquid bubbled, producing gas. Isolation chamber lights blinked in a code. An elaborate system of pressure valves hissed with purpose. Computer screens displayed moving plots of data. An extensive array of heavy knobs with suction grips provided access to all the information. As the Chief Geneticist of Kytim, her mother floated in the middle of it all, her tentacles folded one over another against her chest. "Hub called ahead to tell me you were coming."

"Of course." Hub probably tracked her the whole way and knew she'd end up here before she did. Lexi brushed her hair out of her eyes, a curious human habit she'd picked up, and squared her shoulders. "I'm not going."

Her mother's eye rippled through a series of color fluctuations, from a stark yellow to a burnt orange, indicating surprise mixed with concern. "You're not going back to the drop station today?"

"I'm not going to Colorado. I'm not dropping to the surface. I'm not going through with the mission."

Lexi's mother took a long breath and let it ripple out her side bladders. "Why?"

"You can't fix me, can you? You can't reverse . . ." Lexi ran an oddly formed human limb up and down, indicating her peculiar body. ". . . this."

Lexi's mother visibly drooped under her daughter's gaze. "No, I can't."

Clenching her fists and tensing her whole body, Lexi screamed in frustration. "That is why! I can't win. Even if our mission succeeds, I won't be a hero. I'll be hated. If I come back to live with my own kind, I'll be shunned as an alien. I'll be forever stuck in this bubble with this body."

Her mother's eye rippled into a cloudy violet sorrow, and Lexi felt it too. Tears burned her eyes and coursed down her face. Her mother unfolded her tentacles and wrapped them gently around Lexi's bubble. "I'm sorry, darling."

Lexi folded into herself and lay on the floor of the pod. "Please find a way to change me back, Mom. I want to be Kytimmer again. I want to breathe proper atmosphere. I want tentacles and gas bladders." Sobs shuddered her ridiculous human frame. "I want Daddy back."

The pod speaker keened with her mother's answering grief. "I'm sorry, Lexi dear. I'm sorry." Her mother held her pod and Lexi held herself in the closest way they could hug.

"I can't bring back your father," her mother said between low keens of sadness. "I can't reverse what you have become either. Once we introduced the genetic changes at the end of your larva stage, there was no turning back." Her voice tones vibrated with regret. "I've tried everything. You will be human on the outside for the rest of your life."

Lexi lay back and stared at the scaly flesh of her mother's body and tentacles wrapped around her lonely bubble. One of the tentacles slipped in through the pod portal. Wrapped in latex, it stroked her hair, providing Lexi's only comfort.

Lexi dropped her pod into her assigned deployment station.

"Welcome back, Cadet Lexi," Hub said. "Your make-up assignments are highlighted in your mission file. Please do your best to catch up with your teammates."

Lexi ignored the instructions and opened her private file. She moved a document to the shared server.

"What happened?" Anna's voice emitted through the speaker. "You were gone for a long time."

Lexi looked through the translucent bubble wall and waved to her. Anna answered with a shy wave back.

"I needed a minute."

"Two Earth days is more than a minute."

Lexi shrugged. She'd decided to come back one last time. "I'm sick of Hub's plan. I'm sick of living in this bubble. We shouldn't have to."

Anna's chin tipped upward, straining to look above as if expecting to find something gruesome hanging over her. "What's wrong with it?"

"We deserve better. While I was gone, I made my own plan. If Hub doesn't listen, then I quit."

Anna stared. "You can't quit, Lexi. You're the best."

Lexi turned away and keyed open the com line to the entire team of 300. "Attention Cadets," she spoke in her clearest voice. Being human, it lacked the emotional vibrations natural to the Kytimmer, but human tones had some variations to work with. She used the ones that commanded the most respect. "I've uploaded a file with a revised after-mission plan. Please take a minute to review it." The file flashed as all her classmates downloaded it to their stations.

"It's not time for public announcements, Cadet Lexi," Hub said.

"I don't care. You're going to listen to me. We don't have to live in these bubbles forever." Lexi's voice carried through every pod's speaker. "We will always be human. Chief Geneticist Jymyrizz is my mother. She has discovered it's impossible for us to go back to being Kytimmer after the mission."

Lexi's image flashed across Anna's screen. Anna looked back and forth between the image and her, biting her lip with anxiety. On the other side, Daniel stared at his screen as well. Throughout the entire deployment array, cadets watched her.

Lexi stepped back to show her whole body. "We are stuck like this. But we can be free on Earth's surface."

"That's where we're going," Daniel said.

"I mean for us to live there permanently." Lexi keyed the graphics of her presentation. A section of the third planet's map unfolded. "A human city near my mission assignment was built at over five thousand feet above sea level. There are additional enclaves in the vicinity at six, seven and even eight thousand feet."

The map zoomed in on the province called Colorado, and several places lit up along the irregular topographical features of the region. "We can preserve the atmosphere and ecology of these areas to keep them sustainable for life. We can live there ourselves."

"Cadet Lexi—"

"Shut up, Hub," Daniel said. Several more cadets chimed in with similar sentiments.

"Cadets, please. We have a viable mission plan. These areas have been assigned atmospheric conditions supportive of Kytimmer life, not Earth ecology."

"Let's hear what Lexi has to say," Anna said. More cadets joined the chorus. A handful of the operations engineers turned from their stations to watch.

Lexi keyed the next part of the presentation. A series of data charts and graphics rolled over the screens. Her research had uncovered some interesting circumstances on the third planet. The already precarious nature of its climate made her proposal for atmospheric adjustments easy.

The basic plan still existed. Humans culpable in the Kytim massacre would be brought to justice. The others would spend the rest of their lives in merciful captivity in the lowlands. Lexi preserved the adjustment of the lowland atmosphere to keep the captives docile. Most of the plan to transform the planet to support Kytim's civilization remained the same. The change preserved high-altitude areas for the right mixture of atmosphere for Kytimmer-humans to live. Lexi and her friends could sustain themselves in the highlands and only need their bubbles to travel into the Kytim-like atmospheric bands as needed.

The cadets broke into an excited discussion, talking over the Hub's attempts to bring order. The mission operations specialists downloaded Lexi's files and began their own assessment. A message flashed on Lexi's screen from the office of the Chief Geneticist. She keyed it on, and an image of her mother's radiant eye appeared. The color spectrum rippled across her lens. Varying shades of red, green, and purple revealed the love and pride she felt for Lexi.

"Wow, Lexi. This is quite a plan." Anna stood at the edge of her bubble. "Do you think it will work?"

Lexi joined her and pushed a palm against her bubble's outer skin to touch her friend's hand against the pliable barrier. "It must. We can't live like this. I want us to live our lives together. Even if it must be on the hard dirt of Earth. You, me, and even Daniel. The whole team. None of us will be alone."

Anna's face bloomed into a beautiful smile. "I'd really like that."

Behind them Daniel stomped around in his bubble, gesturing with excitement. All the other cadets jammed the com lines with commentary, each running Lexi's graphics repeatedly.

To the people of Earth, they'd be considered counterfeit humans and the vanguard of doom for an entire planet.

To the Kytimmer, they'd be reminders of a tumultuous time of disaster and change.

To Lexi, they were family.

Collin Irish is an engineer-storyteller. Both halves of his brain get a workout each day. With over twenty-five years of experience as a mechanical engineer he can believably explore the breadth of science fiction from pre-industrial to fantastical technology. He volunteers as a storyteller for youth mentoring groups using mythological imagery for emotional development. He lives in Lakewood, CO, where his wife and two children claim the third half of his brain, and his whole heart. Check out Collin's website, collinirish.com, for more of his writing.

Iphus

Laurel McHargue

"I'm scared, Ellie." Leah's once bright eyes appear sunken. "People are talking about caves and tunnels. It's too late, though, isn't it?"

I gather my wife in my arms. "We have everything we need right here." I remind her of our plentiful rations and secret stockpiles. She squeezes me tighter. She hears what's most important.

"You're right. Our love will see us through whatever happens. And maybe there's still a chance it could shift and pass us by, right?"

"Always a chance." I kiss Leah's forehead and hold her until she releases me.

She walks to a window. Her shoulders slump. I wonder if she believes me.

"Speaking of tunnels, did you hear about the rodent who wants to live in one?" As is our routine, I don't wait for her to answer. "His friends told him to gopher it."

"That's the worst." If only she'd grin. Instead, she gazes into the sky. Along with everyone else on the planet, she watches the approaching sphere. "It's awfully large today."

Large. Close. Imminent. Astronomers eventually identified what we all thought was a blazing comet—"It'll burn out before it hits our atmosphere"—as a rogue planet from a distant galaxy. A planet roughly the size of Earth and ignorant of spatial awareness etiquette. Scientists named it Iphus. A name like a disease.

"At least the news doesn't harp on politics anymore. Silver lining, right?" I try. The planet's approach forces us all to consider how we might focus our days.

Our last days.

Given the reality, I wonder if the decision I'm about to make presents a moral dilemma.

"Remember when we first spotted it?" Leah sounds far away. Lost.

"Yeah. Just a blip in the sky. Another falling star. What did you wish for, babe?"

"Not this."

Absolutely not this. Anything but this.

How could the experts have been so wrong? When faraway islands disappeared two decades ago, global climate change debates still raged. Pundits rehashed what educated people already knew—our planet had weathered ages of temperature fluctuations. It would survive others. It made sense that islands were never meant to be forever, so too bad for fools who bought those properties.

"Where even *are* the Maldives?" I ask.

"*We're* safe."

"Weren't we smart to move to the mountains when we did?"

"Tides'll never reach us."

Tides didn't reach Colorado, but they eventually covered our islands and coastlines. The entire Hawaiian archipelago. Nantucket. Florida. California. Before the first cracks in seaport city skyscraper foundations appeared, before the towers collapsed under their weight into swollen seas, those who could quietly fled inland to higher grounds.

It was good for Colorado until it wasn't. Until the real panic hit. When we knew with certainty Iphus wouldn't veer.

I shuffle to where Leah stands like a statue and kiss the back of her neck. "Know what I wished for?"

"You're not supposed to tell."

"I wished for a long, happy life with the most beautiful woman on Earth." It's a lie. I never wish on falling stars. Leah sinks against me. No longer voluptuous. Years of stress turned both of us bony.

"If I could make a wish now, I'd wish for a *Fifth Element* supreme being to finally feel true love and save us all." Leah's favorite movie. She must have made me watch it a dozen times.

"If only this were just a disaster movie." I hold her. We sway together.

In movies and in reality, a shared crisis can bring out the best in people—a common enemy, a wildfire, a pandemic—but this? How do you work together to thwart a planet-shattering event?

People turned feral.

A few months ago, newscasters stopped pretending. Leah stopped listening. She clung to the maybe-it'll-pass-us-by dream. Pretended to, anyway. For a while.

"Do you wish we'd adopted?" She gazes out into our tiny, fenced yard. Her damp black curls glow an unnatural green. Something in Iphus's approach warps our sun's rays. No one looks healthy in its light. The air smells wrong. Thicker. Sour.

I consider her question. We could have, maybe even should have, adopted. But I was selfish. By the time Leah convinced me we owed more to society than we were giving—she taught middle school and I was our county's Emergency Manager—shit had already hit the fan.

"I wish . . . I wish I'd been braver. I wish we'd had more time. Honestly, I can't imagine what kind of mother I'd be in this situation."

Leah's silent. Doesn't say, "You'd be a great—" Doesn't lie. She knows me too well.

Her silence irks me, but it shouldn't. I never wanted, never needed more than her in my life. Told her that from the start.

She pulls away from me and lowers the shade, casting our tiny kitchen into an even more sinister light. Lower the shade and the threat disappears. She stays there, staring at the glow. "God, it's hot."

Colorado mountain homes never needed air conditioning. As soon as the sun slumps behind mountaintops, temperatures drop abruptly, even in the summer. AC wouldn't help now anyway with electrical grid irregularities. Who could have anticipated a rogue planet interfering with our sun's rays?

With our existence?

"Colorado shouldn't be hot in December." Leah's voice quavers.

"Hey, remember when we used to bitch about having to shovel snow off the sidewalk?" A lame attempt to lighten the mood. Shouldn't have mentioned snow with its associated memories of skiing and skating and hot chocolate by cozy fires—too painful. It stopped snowing here five years ago.

Leah shakes her head, an Etch A Sketch erasing the memories.

"You know what they say about when it gets too hot in the kitchen—"

"Don't."

I want to hold her again, but she's in a bubble. Too fragile in this moment. Signs of her deepening despair frighten me. She loves me, chose me because she believed I'd keep her safe. I'd be faithful. I'd make her laugh.

I'd cure her.

She expects too much.

So did our neighbors until recently.

They used to tease me about my Armageddon mentality. "You read too many apocalypse novels." But when the news became relentless in their catastrophe coverage, friends and acquaintances came to me for advice. Finally appreciated what I did for a living.

"How will this end?"

"Will it be painful?"

"What should we do to prepare?"

How the hell should I know? No Emergency Preparedness Handbook included a chapter on *What to Do in the Event of a Planet Collision*.

So I did my best before the worst of the panic struck. Everyone in our small mountain town—even those without means, we took care of them too—had enough food and water stored to see them through months of economic and supply chain uncertainty.

And I stored extra provisions. Extra things. Things only I would use when I could envision no alternative. Because whatever remains when Iphus hits won't matter. Nothing will matter. It will be the end of matter.

"What do you want for dinner?" Leah's return from her dark bubble startles me from thinking of my extra things. "I know you're tired of beans and rice. I am too. How about a scramble?"

My stomach screams at me. It's pissed I haven't felt like eating in weeks. Months. I should stop watching the news, but that decision will be out of my hands soon. Reception is spotty. And I've seen enough. Scenes of dead, rotting whales and other once-graceful sea creatures litter the land. They can't take the heat either.

Iphus's approach accelerated the already melting polar icecaps. The rapid increase in ocean volume and temperature disrupted breeding cycles and migration routes. Entire aquatic species are saying "fuck it" and throwing themselves to shore. Majestic whales newly impaled on exposed rebar and tangled in the detritus of drowned towns present grotesque landscapes. Still bloated, earlier victims of relentlessly rising tides are ripe for bursting.

I never could stomach the smell of an empty sardine tin in a trashcan. Just the thought of the stench on those horrific, unnatural shorelines raises bile to the back of my throat. But I have to eat something. Can't appear to give up on Leah and her dream. Have to pretend it's just another day, just another decision to make about dinner.

"A scramble sounds perfect. I'll bring in some peas. Hey, you know the difference between popcorn and pea soup?"

She doesn't roll her eyes at me anymore. She just waits.

"You can pop corn, but you can't pea soup." I rush outside before she has time to groan. I hope she groans, it would show some sign of the old Leah, but I know she doesn't bother to do that anymore either. Takes energy she no longer has.

Alone in our pathetic little garden, I consider how it

flourished for a while in the unseasonably warmer seasons preceding the advance of Iphus. And although we're unsure of the long-term repercussions of eating food grown in this bizarre atmosphere, most of us accept there will be no long-term repercussions to worry about.

So we eat our too-green peas to give credit to our labors, leaving stores of canned peas untouched.

Maybe Leah's right. Maybe Iphus will pass us by. Maybe Jesus will save us after all. Isn't that what The Good Book says he'll do at the end of the end times? We've been told it'll be really, really bad, but then he's supposed to save humanity—at least those who've lived righteously—right?

We're supposed to watch for signs. Religious deception, wars and rumors of war, famine, pestilence, earthquakes, signs in the heavens, persecution of the followers of Christ, lawlessness, preaching of the gospel of the Kingdom all around the world. I don't recall anything about a rogue planet, but according to the story, "every eye will see Him." Could Iphus be Jesus in disguise? Wouldn't that be some epic punch line?

From my calculations, the impending collision leaves no time for a plague, though I wouldn't mind a quick swarm of locusts before lights out. Locusts would be great. They'd add some variety to our bland menu.

No one believes the savior story anymore. We're all jaded. Deception? It's ubiquitous. War? Everywhere and endless. Persecution, plagues, preaching, lawlessness, earthquakes . . . yawn. Seen it all. I never did buy the whole you'll-be-in-a-better-place routine. When the Seventh Day Adventists stopped dropping by at dinnertime, I got worried. Even the churches closed their doors a few years ago.

I carry in a small bowl of peas and a few things from storage wrapped in a brown paper bag. "Be right back." I kiss Leah's sallow cheek and whisk the bag into the bedroom. My resolve strengthens.

After dinner, I coax her from the table. "Let's take a walk, babe. Leave the plates. I'll do them later." I've been holding off the inevitable. Leah's depression grows worse each day despite my support and my objectively hilarious jokes. I've failed.

I take her hand and we walk into the miasma.

"It's . . . almost beautiful, isn't it?" She stares at Iphus and I stare at her. She still makes my heart skip.

I hesitate. It's not like I'm dancing a jig over everything's and everyone's imminent demise. But some have found peace in the freedom death will deliver. Freedom from debt, from pain, from fear, from chronic fatigue. From nonsense. I get it.

"Yes. In a weird way, it is beautiful." I'm startled by how much larger the planet looms since yesterday. Emerald and gold swirls whirl around it. Red-orange flames lick its wake. Its anomalous presence makes me dizzy.

We don't walk far before we're covered in sticky sweat.

Leah gazes around at the houses on our block. We're the only ones outside. "What do you think everyone's doing right now?"

"Probably same as we're doing. Being with the ones who are most important."

When neighbors realized they were on their own, that I had no magic wand, no have-these-ten-items-in-a-bugout-bag handout, all attempts at civility ceased. No more freeze-dried Mountain House beef stroganoff meals shared on Friday nights. No more, "Hey, you okay?" when people passed in the street. At least the looting stopped. What was the purpose?

Not long ago, neighbors withdrew.

"You did all you could. More than most. They all know it." Leah squeezes my hand.

"Thanks. That means a lot. Tired?"

My wife stops. She slouches. The beauty has vanished.

"Yeah." A whisper. "I don't want to look at it anymore."

We return to our dreary rooms—I can't think of it as home anymore—and I pour her a warm beer in a glass I'd set out earlier.

Part of the secret stockpile I've hidden from Leah includes my own end times items. My decision is made. I know it's right. When the sleep elixir kicks in, I'll do it.

We sip our drinks side by side, our thighs touching. I ask, "Do you ever wish you'd married someone else? Someone less, I don't know, intense? Someone who didn't crack stupid jokes all the time because she didn't know how else to make things better?" I stare into my glass. I've never before been brave enough to ask.

Leah finishes drinking. She sets down her glass and gently nudges my chin until we're eye to eye. "Never." A drowsy kiss. "You've always done right by me. Don't question yourself now. Not about anything." The sedative works fast. "Anything, you understand?" She slurs, staring into my eyes with an intensity that stops my breath. "I'm tired of bein' afraid. I'm tired, Ellie. Make it go away. Don't wanna see it again. Love you, my funny honey. F'rever 'n' ever."

Does she know?

I carry her to bed.

She's fast asleep in a moment, curled like a kitten in the

spoon of my body. I savor the familiarity of her skin against mine. Just a few more minutes.

I slip away and retrieve a prepped needle.

"I love you, my beautiful dreamer." An old melody plays in my head. I hum through heaving sobs as I inject her. "You don't need to be scared anymore. See? You were right, it's changed course." Maybe she hears me.

It's done. She won't see the planet again.

And I won't let the last sound of Leah's sweet voice be a scream.

Laurel McHargue—a West Point grad raised near Boston—lives and laughs and publishes and podcasts in the breathtaking beauty of Colorado's Rocky Mountains. After years as an Army Officer, a mother of two sons, and an English teacher, Laurel abandoned paid employment to concentrate on her creative Muses. She does her best to keep her darker ones hidden, releasing them only when they scream to tell their tastier tales. A multi-genre author, Laurel writes about life, real and imagined, and hosts the podcast Alligator Preserves. Check out her website at leadvillelaurel.com.

Visited by a Crane

Rick Ginsberg

Mariah watched the standoff between her friend Lexi and the store owner unfold. Their mutual indomitableness evoked both wonder and fear.

"Where'd you get it?" The store owner asked.

"It's mine," Lexi insisted.

"Uh huh." The man examined the coin through the loupe magnifier. "That's not what I asked you. Where'd you get it?"

"Well . . ."

The man peered up from the magnifier and stared at Lexi, waiting.

"Well . . ." She smirked, keeping her eyes on the man, crossing her arms, and blowing at her bangs. "If you must know, the Tooth Fairy gave it to me."

The man scoffed and returned his gaze to the loupe.

"It's true." Mariah chimed in from behind Lexi as she fiddled with the sash belt that hung from the bowline knot at her waist. She was sweating through her tie-dyed shirt.

The store must have had the heat cranked as high as it could go. The sun beamed on Mariah's back from the wide glass windows of the coin shop. Even though it was late March in Denver, it was 85 degrees. On spring afternoons like this, many of the shop owners on the west side of

Broward didn't know what to do to keep their stores comfortable. They struggled with the meticulousness of tailors, alternating between turning on the heat and air conditioning on account of the morning being cold and the afternoon scorching. Mariah imagined the vents smoking as the HVAC unit burned out from indecision, a battalion of bedraggled utility belt-wearing repair techs coming up the street and through the doors cursing climate change.

The man peered intently at the coin. "It's got unusual wear. See this occasionally. It was something important to someone. It was a fetish."

Lexi laughed sharply. "A *fetish?* Creepy."

"Not that kind of fetish." The man frowned as he continued to examine the coin. "They teach you anything at school these days?"

"Yeah," Lexi said as she snickered and rolled her eyes. "Tenth grade is fire."

"It's a talisman."

"Nope. Don't know that one either."

"Something special," Mariah explained, fiddling again with her belt.

"It was my grandmother's. She must have given it to the Tooth Fairy. But you're ruining the whole Tooth Fairy fantasy for me here. That's upsetting. What's next? Santa died?" Lexi still had her arms crossed.

"Uh huh. Sounds like this half eagle meant something special to someone. Maybe your grandmother?" the man asked.

Mariah held her breath while Lexi waited.

He looked up from the magnifier and met Lexi's eyes.

"It didn't," Lexi said.

There was a silence between the man and the girl as they

looked at each other for a long moment. Longer than felt normal.

"Can you Venmo me the money?" Lexi asked.

"I don't do the Venmo."

"*The* Venmo?" Lexi laughed.

"Girls, this is a numismatics store. I deal in cash. And this is a non-reversible transaction. If you change your mind so much as two minutes from now, you'll have to buy it back at mark-up."

"Since you can't use *The Venmo*, we'll take the cash now please." Lexi smirked.

"That was lit! Look at this!" Outside, in the hot spring afternoon, Lexi waved the nine fifty-dollar bills at Mariah. "But that guy. Chrissakes. *Numismatics* shop," she went on, drawing out each consonant. "Ok, Boomer."

"Truth," Mariah whispered as she looked around, afraid someone might be watching.

"Oh, come on. Look what the Tooth Fairy brought us! This is like what, twice what you've raised for the cranes? Four hundred fifty bucks. It's yours." Lexi held the bills out to Mariah.

"Three times, actually."

Mariah slowly started to reach for the bills, but Lexi pulled them back.

"And maybe we take just a little to get ourselves some dank weed?" Lexi grinned. With her free hand she put her forefinger and thumb up to her eye so her iris could just be seen between them. "Just a wee, wee bit, My?" She laughed and repeated herself until Mariah smiled, shook her head, and grabbed the cash.

"Shut up. Okay, let's get high."

I luv Colrudo bcawz uf the Sandhyl Craynz I go cee

—Mariah Maxwell, kindergarten

The girls met the old man fifteen days ago. He was new to the facility, but he was dying, and he told them as much, explaining the concept of hospice.

"They send in the pros when the sand's nearly outta the glass," he told them. "Dying shouldn't be left to amateurs."

The man's skin bore resemblance to a topographical map, complete with crevasses, hills, caverns, and folds of countless colors where memory itself could well be lost. When he squinted to put the oxygen line in his nose or needed more and put an entire mask on his face, his eyes disappeared in rounded wrinkles and his jowls took on the texture and hue of the dry, cracked mud Mariah had seen at her aunt's land up in the Yampa Valley. It was that cracked mud that made her aunt stare out the window, searching for the sandhill cranes amidst the disappearing wetlands and wordlessly passing her worry to her niece. The plight of Colorado's cranes was always with Mariah. It was the true north to the compass of her mind when suffering was concerned.

The old man's body was destroyed, and he knew it.

"Lung cancer," the old man, whose name they learned was Randy, said with a grimace. "Gotta die of something. Don't choose this."

Mariah and Lexi were visiting Randy as the spring

semester of their high school sophomore year wound down as part of their aging and human development class. The girls called it AHud. They had been visiting the nursing home and sitting with residents for an hour at a time for the last eight weeks. Randy would be their last project.

"Smells like piss and bleach in here . . . and a fuck ton of old people." Lexi always commented to Mariah when they entered the nursing home.

The first day, they talked about Randy's career. The dying man was quite proud of his work as an asphalt laborer, constructing Interstate 70 between Idaho Springs and Empire in 1966. He raked and swept the thick road mat and worked the paver and screed machines that flattened and smoothed the ebony road through the forested mountains.

He looked beyond them as if he could see the scenes of his past. "Air so thick with the road, you'd go home with the taste of asphalt in your mouth. Maybe . . . cancer's got to come from somewhere I s'pose. Smokes, too. Lottsa smokes in those days."

And when their hour with Randy was almost finished that first day, he told Lexi and Mariah he wanted to show them something.

"Fella I worked with, a screed machine operator, came back from Korea in 1952 with a bullet in his shoulder. He rubbed it constantly. He was retiring on account of that old shoulder and had taken a liking to me because we talked about the war, the Denver Bears minor league ball club that left in '55, and how pretty it was seeing that road be built. We'd wonder together where it might bring people. Said maybe retirement could let him release the past, his superstitions, demons. Start life fresh. So he gave me his lucky charm. Now it's been mine for almost 60 years."

Randy leaned over to the side table and opened the drawer, withdrawing a gold coin the size of a quarter. He rubbed his thumb on it reflexively, held it in the palm of his worn, cracked hand, and handed it to Lexi.

She grasped it loosely, as though it was contaminated, and quickly turned it over to Mariah who eagerly studied the coin. Liberty profile looking left, 1906, thirteen stars circling her head, its backside a shielded eagle grasping arrows in one talon, an olive branch in the other.

Randy explained to them it was a U.S. liberty head half eagle $5 gold coin, minted in Denver, the first year the mint opened. Ten percent copper alloy, the remainder pure gold.

Mariah had rarely seen such material worth in such a small object, let alone been allowed to touch such a thing. The experience was akin to handling the tooth of a god.

The sandhill cranes of Colorado are in danger. The reason is because the world is getting hotter. They are not use to such warm weather so they might go north and not come back. We need to protect theyr enviriment. If you go to the Yuma Valley you should see the cranes. They are so pretty. You will want to see them again.

—Mariah Maxwell, fourth grade

Mariah's efforts to raise money for the dying and fleeing cranes of Colorado did not begin with the dead crane on her aunt's property. But finding the bird among the browning reeds made it take on a new resonance, the twangs of a tinny child's instrument unfolding into crescendo, albeit sometimes out of tune.

She was eleven, and to escape what was at times the overwhelming nature of friends, school, and her clumsy efforts at gymnastics, Mariah walked alone on the land in the sunny afternoons when her aunt was working on the small farm. She'd hum to herself, closing her eyes and imagining what made the small sounds she heard around her. Sometimes she thought she heard her own heartbeat. But when she opened her eyes, she understood it was something outside and not inside—declaring itself in these small natural sounds. She smoothed that disappointment by thinking about how she could raise money to protect the stunning steel-feathered and red-capped birds.

But one time, when she opened her eyes during one of these moments after walking blind and listening, she saw the crane's wing strangely sticking out of the reeds. Once she got closer, she turned and ran to get her aunt.

Her aunt's face turned grim when she saw the dead bird. She pulled her hands through her graying hair and rubbed her face thoughtfully.

"Come with me."

They returned with a cardboard box. Wearing buckskin gloves, her aunt led the path for both of them through the reeds.

"Can I pick it up?" Mariah asked.

Her aunt stopped and smiled sadly at her niece, then carefully took off her gloves and handed them one by one to Mariah. She pulled them on, though they were far too big, and with the solemnity of a surgeon bent down to get close to the crane. When Mariah picked it up, the dead crane was far lighter than she'd imagined. The bird's long, luminous neck draped over the side of her hand, reminding her of

Play-Doh that had been rolled supple by her warm hands when she was younger.

The crane had not been dead for much more than an hour, her aunt explained.

Alone in her aunt's guest room later, after they had buried the crane, Mariah thought of what that hour was like for the bird, and she counted to herself the seconds for a full sixty minutes as she stared at the ceiling. In the warm room, the bare light bulb cast shadows on the walls. In them she saw the cranes surviving, and along with it a decision that she would abandon the balance beam for the brutality of obstacle course training. At that moment, she yearned for the time when her hands would be calloused.

For half of the price of one latte at Starbucks, you can make sure the threatened sandhill cranes here in Colorado can get the food and environment they need! My name is Mariah Maxwell and I am a 7th grader at Buckley Middle School. I have run bake sales, car washes, sold popcorn, and am trying to organize a 3k road race, all to help the sandhill cranes of the Yuma Valley which are trying to cope with horrible habitat loss. But your donation can further help! All donations will go to Crops for Cranes in the Yuma Valley right here in Colorado. Please consider helping us and be part of the solution, not the problem.

—Flyer distributed door-to-door by Mariah Maxwell

Stop heating up the planet you fucking fucks and killing my cranes!!!!

—Message scrawled in pencil by Mariah Maxwell on one of the undistributed flyers

"Do you know how much that coin is worth?" Lexi asked a few days after Randy had shown them the half eagle.

"How much?"

"That old guy is rolling in the Benjamins with that thing. Hundreds. Maybe more."

The girls were in Lexi's room, on their phones. Occasionally they would look up at each other and share a glance. Mariah felt Lexi trying to catch her eye. The air conditioner hummed.

"We should kill that fuck," Lexi said. "It would be like a mercy killing. You hear all that bullshit about building I-70? Cars just going up and down spewing exhaust. What good did any of that do?"

"Right . . . whatever," Mariah said.

Lexi was silent for a moment.

"Well, look at you. You're fucking swole from your American Ninja shit. You could just put his head in your bicep and, like, I don't know, snuff him out."

"Fuck you." Mariah and Lexi stared down each other until they both broke into loud laughter.

"And we should steal that coin. He doesn't need it. All that money. You could take it. For the cranes."

"I've raised a little. Maybe 150 total."

"Yeah, a little."

"People don't want to give."

"People are wack."

When they returned to the nursing home for their final week, it was unusually cold and drizzly for May. The girls put their jackets on the seat next to Randy's side table.

He was drowsy, not much up for talking, but he told them he could see it was raining outside and asked if there might be a flood, like they were having in New Hampshire.

Mariah's stomach churned thinking how the world was screaming in pain. Not even the lush green hills of New Hampshire could soak up all the rain.

Randy dozed off, his mouth agape. The girls picked up their phones, but then Lexi slid hers into her back pocket and leaned over to the side table. She quietly opened the drawer.

Mariah clenched her jaw as she jutted her head toward Lexi. "No," she mouthed.

Keeping her eyes on Randy, Lexi slid her hand into the drawer. She pulled out the coin, which she quickly dropped down her leggings and into her Ugg boot.

In conclusion, the challenges faced by Colorado's sandhill cranes have almost completely been caused by humans and our bottomless need for lifestyles that consume, create pollution, and cause climate change. It is useful to consider the words associated with another great, human-caused American tragedy when considering the plight of the sandhill cranes not only in Colorado but across the nation. In the 9/11 report it was written, "The most important failure was one of imagination. We do not believe leaders understood the gravity of the threat." We need to imagine what the loss of these great birds would do to our world, and act accordingly.

—Mariah Maxwell, tenth-grade environmental science capstone paper

As Mariah walked the neighborhood her pace quickened, the way it frequently did when she was agitated, and she tried to remember what her aunt once told her about the meaning of being visited by a crane. She couldn't recall, and instead considered that it never really mattered because she didn't need to be visited. She always visited them.

Mariah clenched her fists, her corded forearms tensing as she passed manicured lawn after manicured lawn of vibrant Kentucky bluegrass thriving in the early summer heat of Denver. Her feet met puddles on the sidewalk where thoughtless owners let their sprinklers water the unforgiving concrete, cultivating nothing more than evaporation.

The receptionist at the front desk of the nursing home allowed her to come in even though the class had ended last week, and she made her way to the room. In the hallway, it came to her. If a crane visited you, it meant there would be retribution, justice. And she realized a simple truth as she walked into the room—that the failure of imagination she most often sensed in the world was the inability of older generations to recognize the subjective experience of the younger.

Randy was awake. He pulled off his oxygen mask and looked at her, his face wrought with the woundedness that a lifetime of pains had caused, this betrayal perhaps the worst.

Mariah knew there were no words necessary for what

needed to be done. The cranes would have to wait. She uncrossed her arms and held out her palm. In it shone the small gold coin.

Rick Ginsberg is a writer, consultant, and psychologist who lives in Denver, Colorado. He writes primarily fiction, though his creative non-fiction has appeared regularly in the *Denver Post* and other publications over the last twenty years. He is a former Colorado Voices columnist for the *Denver Post*. Currently, Rick is in the process of publishing his first novel that takes place in the 1980s in coastal Maine. He is also working on a non-fiction book about fathers and their relationships with their children through the game of baseball. His second novel, following the life of a concentration capo in World War II, is in process. Information about Rick and his writing can be found at rickginsbergwriting.com.

Sticka

Natasha Watts

From https://www.sticka.com, archived before the network went down:

BRING THE HEAT
October 5, 2009

My dear readers, when I tell you I am loving the weather this year!

I know, I know, we need it to cool down or we won't get enough snowpack to make up for last winter. Colorado and their snowpack. I know Mr. Sticka grew up here, but these *people* sometimes, I tell ya! As a St. George girlie, this is MY kinda fall. Anyone who tries to convince me otherwise is barking up the wrooong tree.

Lil is loving her full days at school. I try to remind myself it's a Montessori, she needs to socialize, but gosh *dang* is it hard to let go of that sweet girl every morning. I swear it was yesterday she was clinging to my leg while I tried to shove her into nursery so I could go to Sunday School. Like, P*lease, child, let me have two seconds to myself!* And yet now that she's older and I have two other kiddos rubbing their snot on me every second of the day, I can't get enough of her.

Today I took baby Olive and stood outside on the back porch. She was that weird cross between squirmy and clingy, where she keeps trying to get out of my arms and then the second I put her down, she's crying and reaching up for me. So I took her out and we watched birds flitting between the evergreen trees on the hill sloping down from our house, and the two of us were finally still. I felt like it was the first time I've breathed in a long, long while.

Things are the same with my parents. Since I made my big, dramatic post and Mom called to say her piece, they've been radio silent. I don't know if I'll ever forget how she ended our conversation.

"I'll still be me though," I said. I was close to tears at this point and trying to hide it. "This doesn't change who I am, not really. Just what I do on Sunday."

Mom laughed, this weird, short, humorless noise. "Of course, Sticka (except she said my real, full, baby-blessing name). You'll be you, but you know this isn't just about Sundays, right? Families are forever *only* if every member lives true to their eternal covenants."

Good Girl Sticka has never come as close to saying an actual swear word in front of her mother. I wanted to curse that woman out. I should have! But I don't do that. Instead, I filed it away for the blog, a place where YOU, my wonderful readers, accept every inch of my imperfect, messy, un-eternal self.

What do you think? Any favorite swears I should put into rotation now that I'm a heathen?

203 COMMENTS

IT'S PRETTY MUCH THE NOTEBOOK, Y'ALL
October 6, 2009

Do you wanna hear a love story?

Ten years ago, a young, silly girl in college ding-dong ditched the wrong apartment. She was trying to get her brother's new place, but she had the number wrong. A serious, quiet boy opened the door instead.

"Who are you?" he asked. His eyebrows were very thick and very emotive.

The girl took three long seconds to remember how to talk. Even then, it came out like, "'m Sticka."

And so that name was born, from my inability to say "I'm Jessica, a very mature and attractive young woman who would never ding-dong ditch" in front of the cute boy who is now my husband and the father of my three children. If only the two of us knew everything that would follow in the next decade. Would we have been scared? Excited? Mr. Sticka claims he would have run screaming, but I can't see it. He was never much of a runner.

I certainly never could have guessed I'd be sitting in pajamas on a Tuesday afternoon, typing out my random thoughts to thousands of readers that care about what I have to say for some reason. What are you people doing?! I have no idea what's going on!!

You're still here? Well, in that case, prayers (or good thoughts or positive energy) it stays warm enough to take the kids to the lake this Saturday. Mr. Sticka has grudgingly agreed to a family paddleboat rental! Doesn't that sound just perfect?

What are your plans for this summery October weekend? [Edit: Keep it civil in the comments, ladies, sheesh. I've never had to moderate them before, but I will if you make me!]

399 COMMENTS

PANIC AT THE COSTCO
October 8, 2009

A phone conversation with my husband, with occasional interruptions from CNN and Caden:

Him: Hello?

Me: Pick up some diapers, if you can find them. I'm not switching to cloth even if the world ends.

Him: They're out of diapers.

Me: . . .

Caden: Moooom! My ball fell in the creek again.

Me, a picture of maternal grace: Well, I guess it's gonna live there now! (In my defense, the creek bed has been nasty lately from all the standing water.)

Him: Wait, I found some off-brand diapers on top of the shelf.

Me: And THAT's why I married a tall man.

CNN: *The whole world has fallen into a deep drought. It will never rain again and we're all gonna die.*

Him: Anything else?

Me: Did you get the cream cheese? I can't make my Crack Chicken without it.

Him: I wish you'd stop calling it that.

Me: It is like crack. I am addicted to it. GET ME MY CRACK.

(Recipe at the end! It's literally that good.)

CNN: *Are you panicking yet? BUY OUT ALL THE WATER AT COSTCO IMMEDIATELY OR YOUR FAMILY*

WILL DIE. THE WORLD IS ENDING.

Me: Yes, we know, Anderson Cooper! EVERYBODY KNOWS, now can you chill out for a second?

Me: Get some water, too.

Him: We have a well, Sticka. We'll be fine.

Sticka's World-~~Famous~~-Ending Crack Chicken

2 lbs boneless skinless chicken thighs (I trim off every last bit of fat)

1 packet ranch seasoning

2 packages cream cheese

Crumbled bacon (you can fry your own, or I like this stuff from Costco)

1 cup shredded cheese

Freeze dried scallions for topping (I used to use fresh, but have you seen those prices lately?? No thanks.)

Throw chicken, seasoning, and cream cheese in the crockpot on low for 6-8 hours. Shred, then top with the bacon and cheese. Once that's melted, serve it over rice or on buns with scallions on top. Take a bite, go to heaven, etc., etc.

315 COMMENTS

ALLOW ME TO GET SAPPY FOR A SECOND ...
October 14, 2009

Did I really abandon you for six whole days?? You understand, of course, with everything going on right now.

I know I like to keep it light here, and I promise I'll get back to your regularly scheduled Sticka soon enough. But in these unprecedented times, I find myself prompted (is that even the right word anymore?) to focus on gratitude.

I have a complicated relationship with gratitude. Growing up in the Church, it was something we expressed directly to Heavenly Father for what he's blessed me with. Now that I'm a little more unsure about the nature of God and prayer and why good or bad things happen to me, who am I thanking when I show gratitude?

Still, I feel compelled to be grateful. Without it, I'm not sure what else to cling to. So here goes.

I'm grateful for our well. I know many of you are in cities that have started to ration drinking water. My heart goes out to you. When we moved to this house three years ago, I had no idea how essential that well was going to be. Even now, we're having to let our poor lawn go brown. But I can't imagine not having the well at all!

I'm grateful that I just weaned Olive off breastfeeding. I was torn about whether it was right (hello, mommy guilt!), but now I'm just relieved because who knows how my supply would have held up? The stress of the past few days, combined with the possibility of not being able to fully hydrate? I genuinely don't know if I could have kept her fed.

I'm grateful for more time with my kids. I'll be honest, I can struggle with this! I counted on those half days when Caden and Lil were both at school. They were these precious, quiet moments with baby Olive that I didn't realize I should treasure until they were gone. But now, in between Caden's disaster messes/injuries (you know how he is), I'm trying to focus on the good. Like today, when I walked in on Lil singing Olive back to sleep during her nap. I'd heard the baby cry and was coming to comfort her, but when I walked down the hall, the door was already cracked. I watched my sweet, beautiful girls and was overwhelmed with a sense of peace that felt like a long drink of water after the chaos on the news the last few days.

I know it's a scary time, but what's getting you through it? What are you grateful for?

121 COMMENTS

WHAT TO DO DURING "EXCEPTIONAL DROUGHT"
October 16, 2009

Take short showers with a bucket on the floor to preserve water. NO BATHS, even for the baby.

If it's yellow, let it mellow. If it's brown, flush it down.

Wash dishes by hand.

Go full pioneer and wash LAUNDRY by hand. I made this [adorable DIY washboard](#) that Amanda posted over on her blog. It almost makes the chore fun! Key word: almost.

Let your cars get dirty. Mr. Sticka hates this one! Our house is up a dusty road, so he usually goes to the car wash twice a week. Sorry, Charlie.

Let your grass and flowers die, even if it hurts your heart.

I know all you lovely readers are used to recipes and updates on my little gremlins, but with all this craziness, I'm considering a change of tone for the blog. Would you all stick with me if I did that? Some of you have been with me for seven years now, and goodness knows the blog looks different now than it did then. I hadn't even had Lil yet! There wasn't even the mommy part of the mommy blog!

Lately I'm having a hard time focusing on the little day-to-day mom stuff. Mr. Sticka's siblings in Idaho have just had to evacuate their families because of the Piney Peak and

West Terreton fires. They've managed to get safely to his parents' property out in Boise, but communication has been scarce because the frequent power outages mean they can't often charge phones or use the internet. I'm honestly surprised we haven't had any outages yet over here. I guess we should be able to use the generator Mr. Sticka went and bought right before the shortage, so that's good.

It may sound silly to some, but it's important to me that I keep you updated. Even though I've never met you in person, you're like another family to me, especially through all this stuff with my parents. Barring any crazy emergencies, I plan to keep writing posts, even if they become a little more "How To Survive the Apocalypse" than before.

With state borders starting to get shut down and wildfires blocking highways, it's easy to feel alone and helpless right now. I have no idea what the future holds, but I think we all know this isn't something that's going to magically get fixed in a day. There's a hard road ahead of us. I realized that later than some people. And I'm scared, but I'm a tiny bit less scared than I could be because I have all of you.

89 COMMENTS

IT'S GONNA TAKE A LOT (TO DRAG ME AWAY FROM YOU)
October 17, 2009

I bless the rains down in EVERGREEN!

You guys remember that old Toto song? My dad used to play the album all the time on Saturday mornings. I have so many memories of him in the kitchen making waffles or in the garage showing me how to maintain the lawnmower while this blared at maximum volume from our boombox.

I can't help but wonder what he's doing right now. It's 8 AM as I'm writing this, which is when he used to get me up despite all my moaning and groaning about how he's ruined my one morning to sleep in. He'd fling open the curtains and bellow that "Oh, What a Beautiful Morning" song. I never thought I'd miss that.

Somewhat related: I tried calling my parents for the first time since The Conversation. They haven't replied to my voicemail.

In any case, back to the RAIN!!

Out of nowhere, it started pouring buckets yesterday. I'd almost forgotten what rain felt like! I know I'm a desert girl, but after sooo long without it, I'm not about to complain. Even though it's caused some crazy unexpected consequences.

Apparently after a drought, sudden rain can actually cause floods! Who knew, right? The creek by our house that was pretty much gone has now straight-up flooded the ONE road out of our little mountain neighborhood. So we're stranded for the time being.

I wouldn't be too concerned, except our saving grace this entire time—our well—has been having issues.

Last night, Lil kept staring at her cup of water during dinner (mashed potato pearls and mac 'n cheese, *très* gourmet).

"Ew, Mommy."

"Hmm?" I was on the floor, cleaning up the plateful of mac 'n cheese Caden had just dropped.

"I want new water."

I went over to look, but it was hard to tell because it was

in a blue plastic cup. I poured it into a clean glass and, sure enough, the water had a brown tint to it! Pretty sure I gagged.

Mr. Sticka says it's probably just tannin, whatever that is. The heavy rain washed it into our well, but it's fine to drink. I'd definitely prefer to get it tested or something, but with the road blocked, we're gonna have to wait for that.

There's not a cloud in the sky now, which is pretty crazy, but I'm hopeful that this could be a turning point with the water shortage. Send good thoughts/energy/prayers that we'll get enough rain to put out some of those wildfires down south, too! The smoke has been HORRIBLE.

Have you had any rain where you live? I know some of you have been getting cut off from the World Wide Web, but I so appreciate anyone who's still hanging in there! We'll get through this together.

64 COMMENTS

[UNTITLED POST]
December 3rd, 2009

It's been a long time. After what's happened, I didn't think I would ever come back to the blog. I still don't know if I will, but I have to write this down. I have to come to terms with the fact that it's real.

On this day six years ago, I went into labor with my second child. It wasn't sudden and dramatic, like my water breaking in the middle of a baseball game with Liliana. We weren't even sure I was in labor this time until the nurse measured me and I was dilated to seven inches. It took ages to progress after that, a full night and through the next day before the doctor told me I was allowed to push. And then suddenly, out the baby came, easy as pie.

Like all our pregnancies, we had waited to find out the gender. Mr. Sticka—Peter—was the one to proclaim, "It's a boy!" He was thrilled. I was terrified. I didn't know what to do with a boy. I'd had no brothers, no male friends growing up. He was a scrawny thing. We named him Caden, because it meant strength.

I'd sometimes wonder after the fact if that was a mistake, because Caden grew into the name in the most chaotic way possible. He never knew his own strength, always accidentally knocking things over and playing too rough with the other kids. He had such a gentle spirit, never meant to hurt a fly, but he didn't know how to turn down the volume on his own body. He was loud and clumsy and got into trouble a lot.

But he was perfect, so, so perfect. I wish I would have told him every single day how perfect he was.

After my last post in October, our family got sick. Lil was the first to complain of a tummy ache. Then myself and baby Olive came down with fevers. Peter got a mild version, but the rest of us were having horrible, horrible diarrhea for days.

My little boy, my Caden, was the last to come down with it. We thought he would luck out, but when it hit him, it came on stronger than it did with anyone else. He had a raging fever, could barely leave the bathroom, and his stomach cramps were so bad he would vomit from the pain. Every hospital I called was slammed. The one nurse I could get on the phone told us to stay hydrated and ride it out.

I still can't write the details of what happened next. It happened so suddenly. He declined faster than anyone could have anticipated, and the flooding on the road was so bad no ambulance or car could make it in or out. Peter tried to carry Caden across at one point, in a desperate attempt to get to the main road and then hitchhike to a hospital, but the current was too strong. He had to turn back less than halfway through.

Caden John Wilbert passed away in my arms on October 30th, 2009. The illness was violent and terrible, but in the end he was still and tired and so, so frail. He felt like a fallen leaf in my arms, like if I squeezed too hard in my grief he might crumble.

We buried him in the yard, under the tree where he had started—but never finished—building a treehouse with his father. Today would have been his sixth birthday.

I once read a journal entry from someone who had lost a loved one, though I can't remember who. They had only written, "The light has gone out of my life."

I have no words of my own to describe this pain. I no longer feel like I exist in my body. Peter has managed the care of the girls, the house, nursed us to health as fires threaten evacuation almost weekly. I have hardly walked or spoken since we buried my sweet boy.

The light has gone out of my life.

15 COMMENTS

[UNTITLED POST]
December 7th, 2009

Hey, everyone. This is Peter. Some of you might know me as Mr. Sticka.

Jess asked me to update the blog. You're all important

to her, almost like family. Despite the obvious reasons why she hasn't been able to regularly update anymore, she's decided she can't leave you completely. So I'll link to a few highlights from the blog, memories from when things were better, posts that you all seemed to enjoy a lot. She hopes they give you some light in what is a hard, hard time for many in the country right now. I know they did for me.

<u>THAT TIME I DECIDED TO BE GOOD AT HALLOWEEN</u>
<u>HEIRLOOMS (TOMATO AND OTHERWISE)</u>
<u>THANKS FOR THE MEMORIES</u>

8 COMMENTS

[UNTITLED POST]
December 11th, 2009

Peter again. Another one from the archives for you today.

<u>CADEN WILBERT, 4-YEAR-OLD SUPERHERO</u>

3 COMMENTS

AN UPDATE
December 16th, 2009

It's Peter. I finally figured out how to title these things. Jess wanted me to give a quick update for anyone still reading. We are hanging in there. The road is finally unblocked, so if we have to evacuate, we'll have a way out. We have enough gas to get out of immediate danger. She thinks of you often and hopes you've all escaped the worst of this.

8 COMMENTS

CHRISTMAS EVE ANGER
December 24th, 2009

Growing up, I sat through countless lessons in Church about the prodigal son. I feel a bit like him, coming back to this blog. Except there's no fatted calf waiting for me, because less than a quarter of the country even has access to the internet anymore. I'm as shocked as anyone that *we* still do.

I think about my readers every day. I hope you're safe. I hope your children and loved ones have been safe. I wouldn't wish this pain upon anyone, even the person who left their grocery cart in the parking lot that <u>I hit with Mr. Sticka's new car that one time</u>.

It feels so weird to make a joke. I used to write like that all the time. Now it's like channeling an entirely different person.

It's Christmas Eve, obviously, and I've been doing a lot of thinking. I have so much anger about what happened—what's still happening. I'm angry at my parents for not answering my calls, even though now I'm pretty sure it's not because they don't want to. I have no idea if they're okay, which makes me scared, which always morphs back into anger. I'm angry at God, if he's even up there. I'm angry that I can't fix what's going on in the world, that I can't take away this pain before it happens somewhere else. I can't remove anyone's cup from them, and no one can remove this cup from me. And that makes me *rage*.

The thing is, I'd rather be angry than nothing at all. I have had nothing at all inside me for two full months. I can do something with angry.

0 COMMENTS

THIS IS A POST ABOUT LEAVING
January 1, 2010

. . . in two senses of the word. I write this from the bed of a run-down motel, unshowered because the water is off, $20 poorer because the owner was desperate for any tenants at all. Peter is out looking for our dinner, because we had no time to pack food before we fled our home.

Our home—I'm trying not to be dramatic, but I know we'll never see it again. The house we renovated, that we turned into our dream home to raise the children. The place where the view goes for miles over the conifer-capped peaks of the Front Range, making me feel tiny and gigantic all at the same time. The place I brought home baby Olive to. The place where I buried my son.

The wildfires finally came, and with a hungry quickness that startled us despite our preparations. We watched the smoke grow closer and threw everything we could grab into the car. We took too long, even then. Ten minutes into the drive, the trees on either side flanked us in flames. I had a moment in my heart where I had to consider the possibility we wouldn't make it. Then we were through the worst of it, speeding toward a town in north Colorado I won't disclose. I'm not sharing because we're hoping to cross the border tomorrow. We'll take a mountain pass road that's closed in the winter but that we've heard might be unblocked because the Department of Transportation is too busy with other disasters to worry about the normal machinations of the day-to-day. If we're able to take that road, our next gamble is that there is no border checkpoint where this particular path crosses into Wyoming, unlike all major highways that link us to our neighbor state.

Our final gamble is that my parents are still in Laramie, and that they're willing and able to shelter us now that our own refuge is gone. There haven't been any major fires in their area, as far as I can tell, but there is so much else that can have gone wrong. In every quiet moment my mind races through them, all the reasons they haven't been able to call me back. Of course, there's still also the chance they've *chosen* not to, but I can't find it in myself to be worried about that anymore. I've been too scared or proud or hurt to reach out since they found out I left the Church. But everything that has happened has taught me that these people are my family. We have no one else in a radius of 100 miles who we could go to, and so we go to them.

I don't know if anyone will ever read this. But I needed to post, to leave a record that we were here, and that we're not giving up. I hope you're not giving up either.

1 COMMENT

Natasha Watts is a writer and audio producer living in the foothills of the Rocky Mountains. She is co-editor of Colorado Book Award finalist *Wild: Uncivilized Tales* and has work featured in *Leading Edge Magazine*, *Bizarre Bazaar*, and *Found*. As Tasha Christensen, she publishes the *Itaska High* romantic comedy series for teens. In her free time, she enjoys listening to podcasts, getting lost in virtual reality, and going on outdoor adventures with her husband and daughters. Find her at NatashaWatts.net and TashaChristensen.com.

The Cistern

Mark Stevens

When you move out of the city, you stop taking water for granted. Particularly, like us, if you are half off the grid. We have electricity, but our water is hauled in by truck. About every three weeks we need 1,000 gallons. The water is funneled through a pipe into an underground cistern. A pump and a pressure tank take care of the rest.

We have three rain barrels connected to our gutters. They fill during a storm or when the snow melts off the roof. We fill plastic pitchers while our shower water heats up. We use that to make coffee, fill Arlo's water bowl, and water the indoor plants. We don't let water run while doing dishes. Our showers are no longer places for meditation. As a writer, I miss long showers with my head deep in a problem with a plot.

Out here in the country, I have a relationship with water. I feel more connected to the environment. Water management is a trade-off.

The private road to our house curlicues up over a mile to where we live, on the top of a knoll. Nobody would look at the modest house and say "trophy." But we have knockout views of our valley in western Colorado.

About halfway up the road is a monitor-style barn. We turned the upstairs "loft" in the barn into a cozy studio apartment. The space rents for $225 a night. The money helps. After all, $225 is more income than I've earned from writing in the past 18 months. Sure, I've had success, but that was a big injection of cash twenty years ago.

I've been short of ideas and the market sucks and my agent doesn't call me back. Oh, and I've been saying "we" but the truth is my wife is taking "a break" from our marriage. I've been a bit of a grouch. Of late.

When we converted the upstairs loft to an apartment, we installed a second cistern at the barn. The 1,750-gallon cistern came with two lids like giant radiator caps. You need both lids because when it comes time to clean, you want good airflow so you don't feel like you're cleaning a claustrophobic crypt. The lids have to be tightly secured. Unfortunately, our installer forgot to make sure the interior of the cistern was ventilated. Without vents, the pressure increases as the water goes down and turns the thing into a giant vacuum.

The first big rainstorm after our new cistern was installed didn't happen for four months. The storm turned the water in the barn apartment into an unappetizing muck.

That was on the first night of a week-long booking. We lost $1,575 and gained a mean-spirited online review.

We tried tracking down the installer, but that individual was about as absent and unreachable as my literary agent.

So cleaning the cistern, given how much time I had on my hands, fell to me.

Besides, I figured, I could use the time to think.

Or perhaps *not think*. I've found that the best ideas come to me when I'm kind of zoned out, like I was when I used to take those long city showers.

"I'm telling you, it's so low-risk it's like some kind of joke."

Vince isn't sure why he needs Bobby Means along on this ride. On this idea of his. But he could use the extra eyes, ears, and hands.

"He'll remember you," says Bobby.

"A guy like that? We were the cheap labor hauling rocks in wheelbarrows. That asshat never came out to talk to us. *Mr. Artist*."

"Artist?"

"Writer. One of his books got made into a movie. With Jeff Bridges. There's a poster in his living room. Dude's got money."

Bobby Means slumps in his rickety wicker armchair, a prize he scavenged from the town dump. He strikes a match and touches the flame to a joint so small it looks like he's lighting his lips on fire. He takes a puff. The exhaled smoke races off, courtesy of a gale whistling through the cracks of the beat-up trailer.

"We're burglars now?" says Bobby.

"You couldn't use some easy money?"

"Nobody uses cash anymore."

"We're bound to find something."

Bobby's trailer sits within view of the highway, on the crusty rundown edge of Cortez.

"You said it's at the end of a long road. Up high." Bobby wears a black T-shirt with a tattered American flag across his skinny chest. *Stomp on my Flag and I'll Kick Your Ass*.

"So?" says Vince.

"So if there's only one way out and if someone comes

home, we're trapped."

"We drive up, scope it out. If there's no answer, we're golden."

The skunky marijuana cloud doesn't hide the smell of cat pee, but there are no cats. Dirty dishes and cans of Old Milwaukee overflow from the sink like an avant-garde sculpture. When it comes to Bobby claiming to be some kind of flag-waving patriot, Vince wonders if Bobby has ever paid one dime in taxes.

Vince sips on a warm Miller Lite. It's 10:30 a.m.

Buddies since high school, took auto mechanics, got crappy grades, and had no future. Two years after not graduating and two years of complaining about work on the farm, Bobby got nailed with a DUI. He'd been speeding on his motorcycle. The fines set him back. He tried fighting the ticket. The lawyer cost him even more. He lost. He picked up a job helping at an auto body shop to pay his fines and bills. It was a month before the pandemic hit. The generous unemployment checks were like winning the lottery. Bobby Means wanted the pandemic to last forever.

When that gravy train dried up, he found work at a tire shop. He fell in with a group that believed the election of 2020 was stolen. A fight with a customer over The Big Steal resulted in a fresh set of walking papers. Bobby fell deeper into the angry crowd. He branded himself as a victim. He crammed into a van for the long ride to Washington, D.C. claiming he would help "get the whole damn country back on track."

Bobby returned with tales of being inside the Capitol. He had crawled in through a smashed window and chanted with the crowd about hanging Mike Pence. But he hadn't hurt a cop or damaged property. The government sent out an investigator for an interview. Bobby's borderline behavior at the Capitol warranted a newspaper story, and Bobby said a few dumb things about government waste and inefficiency before his lawyer told him to say nothing.

Vince had listened to Bobby's stories about the trip with impatience. Bobby wanted credit like he'd walked on the moon. He bragged about not getting prosecuted by the government. He called the investigators "boneheads." Vince hated the idea that Bobby rode for months and months on pandemic check handouts and didn't see the irony in his hatred for the government.

"When I was working up there at that writer's house," says Vince, "we were told we could just whiz in the woods. They get all their water brought in on a truck—so they didn't want us flushing toilets. I made up an excuse to use the bathroom inside because I was dying for a break in the air conditioning. Plus, I wanted to see how this jerk lived."

"Maybe you didn't notice him paying attention."

"Even if he remembers me, the point is we get out of there if he's home. And I'm telling you, inside that home?" Vince whistles, shakes his head. "There's plenty."

"Computers ain't worth shit," says Bobby. "Nothing's worth anything. And what if he's home?"

"We say we got the wrong place and that's that."

"And what if the place is locked?"

"Out in the country? Places like that? He has like three decks and a whole bunch of side entrances. Plus it's summer and if nothing else you know there's going to be windows wide open."

Cleaning the cistern didn't bother me. At least, in theory. I liked the concept of the work. I needed to get out of my routines, which involved skulking about the house, making up excuses not to write, and prowling about the internet looking for a plot or a character to latch onto and get my writing groove back.

First, I loaded supplies. Ladder, drinking water, phone, sump pump, shop vac, extension cord, socket wrench and sockets for the bolts on the lid, a ham sandwich and a cold IPA in a small cooler, two Milk Bones, Arlo's water bowl, and Arlo. All went in an old pickup I keep for running errands in town, when I want to fit in like one of the locals. I know the truck doesn't really fool anyone. The true locals all know each other.

They don't trust newcomers. They think newcomers want to destroy their way of life. In fact, my short-term rental property is just the kind of thing they can't stand—the outside world coming in to jack up real estate prices, bring their art galleries and their sushi restaurants, and wipe out all the places available for red-blooded Americans to rent. I am the problem.

I drove down to the barn on our washboard dirt road. Arlo bounced in the pickup bed in back. The trip takes three minutes. The truck barely gets above five mph, but Arlo likes to stick his head into the breeze and pretend he's going ninety.

Arlo is a chocolate lab with a chill disposition. He's ten. Sleeping is his raison d'être. Writing, of course, is mine. But how do you write when you can't find the thread? I'm known for my gritty crime fiction. One critic compared me to James Crumley. Not sure about that, but it sure felt good. Still, who knows James Crumley today other than us crime fiction aficionados? Who knows me?

I parked the truck by the barn in the hot sun. I unbolted both cistern lids and peered down into the murky soup. Arlo watched me work for a few minutes and then sized up the general scale of my project and decided it would be a long day. He found a spot in the shade for a snooze.

I lowered a sump pump and listened to its throaty gargle as it sucked dirty water from the plastic tank. The water pooled in the stubby driveway by the barn apartment before carving its own creek and heading off into a patch of parched scrub oak that no doubt appreciated the random gift. The barn driveway turned to mud, but a couple days of our hot sun would return the surface to its natural concrete consistency. Every plant, tree, weed, and shrub within 200 miles was parched and suffering.

In fact, I couldn't stop thinking about writing a novel about water wars in the west. Something a bit futuristic. A prediction of sorts. In fact, thinking about "My Water Novel" as I called it to myself, is what was preventing me from writing another one of my gritty, realistic crime novels. I've written seven such novels, one of which was made into an okay movie starring a few well-known actors. The movie rights covered about ten years of my normal writing income, but then that money dried up. So to speak. And one doesn't rest on one's laurels.

When the sump pump had finished its work, there was still about three inches of tenebrous liquid left in the bottom of the cistern. To make matters worse, the floor of the cistern's interior isn't smooth. It's a series of molded polyethylene square pockets. Picture a giant waffle with each square about the size of a slice of toast. Instead of a smooth bottom surface, it was like having several hundred mini-pools of dirty water. This would be my Moment of

Zen, the mind-deadening task of going pool by pool with my shop vac slurping out water from these compartments.

I rigged an extension cord from the barn and carried my shop vac to the closest of the two hatches. I lowered a stepladder into the cistern. I took off my sneakers and socks and put on my Tevas. On the first trip down into the tank, I took the shop vac.

I quickly realized a major problem. Once the shop vac filled with water, it was too heavy to lift back up the ladder. So the shop vac had to remain above, outside the cistern, and I hoped the hose and its extension would reach all the fussy pockets, especially those in the dead center of the tank between the two hatches. If not, I would need to buy a bigger and better shop vac that would reach farther into the brown gunk, much like I was trying to force my brain to dig deeper for better ideas in the squishy matter between my ears.

I'm a writer. I can spot metaphors a mile away.

The interior footing was slick. I lifted the ladder out of the hole so it was out of my way. I was just tall enough to reach the ladder and pull it back down when the time came, provided no coyote or bear came along and dragged it away when I wasn't looking. If that happened, I wasn't sure if I would have the arm strength to pull myself up and out on my own.

What I really had to do, however, was to let myself disappear into the task. I needed to stop thinking about each stupid step.

I needed to find the right headspace where my brain opened itself to new possibilities and ideas.

You can't sit at a table and *think harder* when you're blocked. You need to almost go the other direction, like you haven't got a care in the world.

"I got twelve dollars and I sure ain't spending it on gasoline," says Bobby.

They are at a Conoco at a wide spot in the highway, three miles from the long road that leads up to the writer's house. The gauge is dead on E. It's been that way for the last 20 minutes, but all Bobby has done is laugh about how worried Vince is that they might run out of gas.

"We'll stuff our pockets with cash at his house," says Vince.

"How much have you got?" says Bobby.

"I'll chip in five, you put in five—that's two gallons. Enough to get us up to his house and back all the way to your place."

Bobby's ride is a two-door 1990 Nissan Truck with a bench seat. Around the big-ass pickup trucks of southwestern Colorado, it's a clown car. Bobby's truck is orange. And rust.

"Hell," says Bobby. He pulls out one crumpled five-dollar bill from his blue jeans pocket. Vince takes it, goes inside, and asks the cashier to put seven dollars on Pump 4. The needle sits between E and L when they pull out.

"You ever notice the price of gasoline is the same at all the stations?" says Bobby. "Price goes up a nickel at one, goes up a nickel at the next. Everything is rigged. Every goddamn little thing."

"If you think everything's a conspiracy, then what's the point?" For a stoner, Bobby complains about everything.

"What do you mean?" says Bobby.

"If everything is a conspiracy, then it doesn't matter

what you do, your fate is sealed. Somebody else is in control. Always. Did you even vote?"

Bobby says nothing.

"See?" says Vince.

"The truth will come out," says Bobby.

Bobby wrestles the steering wheel. They are on a steep pitch.

"You can make up anything," says Vince.

"You don't read what I read."

"You mean Reddit?"

Bobby once had enough money to buy a decent phone. Vince believes Bobby's parents pay the bill to keep tabs on their son.

"Don't tell me what I can't read."

"You can read anything, as long as you don't *believe* everything."

"Shut up," says Bobby.

"Do you really think it was a good idea to, let's say, *hang* Mike Pence? Like, live on TV? For real?"

Bobby shrugs. "The president said he wanted us there."

"The president who *lost* the election."

"It would have been pretty cool." Bobby puts the gear shift in neutral, taps the brakes. Their turnoff is coming up. "It didn't happen."

The shop vac makes a horrendous sound. When I had imagined the work on my Zen-like task, I thought it would be peaceful. Perhaps serene. There was no such chance with the racket from the shop vac, like a soprano jet engine in pain.

I worked from one end toward the middle. When the

extension hose reached its limit, I planned to climb out, move the ladder to the second hatch, and start all over again from the other side.

Finally, I decided on a full break. I pulled the ladder down into the hatch, climbed out, drank some water, and ate half a sandwich. I sat in the shade of the barn, on the ground. Arlo wandered over to inspect for crumbs. I gave him a scrap of bread from my palm.

Arlo sat briefly by my side, then went down on his side, his warm body touching my sweaty legs in as many places as possible.

"What's it like not to have a care in the world?"

Arlo said nothing.

My body didn't want to restart. It wanted the other half sandwich. It wanted to join Arlo in a snooze.

"You're not helping," I told Arlo. "You're not helping at all."

I forced myself back into the harsh sunshine and back down the ladder.

Bobby steers the truck onto a long dirt straightaway. The washboard surface rattles the Nissan like they are in the world's most prolonged earthquake.

"You don't know what I'm reading," says Bobby. "You're the one who is *choosing* to stay ignorant."

"That crap gets *debunked*. There's like fact checkers at regular websites. There is truth. You know that, right?"

"You believe the lamestream media?"

"You've let all these voices into your head, Bobby. You're choosing to live in a place where the world is all rigged and you're the dupe—the pathetic *victim*—unless you join the crusade. You want to be the victim? Does it feel good?"

"I'm supposed to follow you as some kind of role model?"

Since not graduating from high school five years earlier, Vince has tried just about everything—driving trucks, driving forklifts, and working on light carpentry, washing windows, and the landscaping crew.

"My world is simple. And it comes with a girlfriend." Vince knows this is crossing the line. Bobby has never had a relationship. "Karla lives in the real world, too."

"Jesus," says Bobby. "You're Mr. Respectable? Think Karla is going to think the world of you when you get arrested for stealing from this writer dude? What about cameras up here? Did you ever think of that?"

"I looked," says Vince. "There's no cameras. This is a quick trip to close a bit of the wealth gap, that's all. It's lower-risk than riding in this death trap."

Through the driver's side window, Vince spots a small barn with a pickup truck out front. He doesn't recall the barn at all. It wasn't in his head the hundred times he's thought through this scenario.

"It's still a half-mile up to the house," says Vince, anticipating Bobby's worries. "And I don't see anybody anyway."

Inside the cistern, the noises from the outside world are dampened and muffled. But the roar of that engine, which was kind of high-pitched and whiny, left no doubt there was somebody on the road.

My road.

We get delivery trucks up here, of course. UPS and FedEx. We also get people who are lost. The road signage isn't all that precise and GPS can get whacky, sending out-of-towners astray.

Of course we also get the renters coming to stay at our apartment above the barn, but I had used the online dashboard to make the listing unavailable due to maintenance.

I poked my head out of the hatch. I saw a funny-looking orange pickup truck that rode low to the ground and didn't appear to be enjoying the climb. Sunlight blasted the windshield. I saw two guys in the cab, so small there was no room for a third. The driver, closer to me, glanced at the barn. He didn't spot me. He would have to know where to look because I had to stand on tiptoes to see out. Plus, a thicket of wildflowers cluttered the view. I pegged the pair as early twenties, on the scruffy side. I'm not judging, but there are lots of people out here who are in survival mode from high school on. These guys looked like that.

Given the funky state of their wheels, they weren't going far. Again, metaphor alert. A cheap one. Don't hate me.

Arlo lifted his head from his prone position in the shade by the barn, ran an internal analysis of the pros and cons of getting agitated, and opted not to expend any unnecessary energy.

I ran my own calculations. Three minutes up, a couple minutes to figure out nobody was home or that they had the wrong place, and three minutes back to my location. Eight minutes. If they didn't return in eight minutes, I would climb out of the cistern and drive the truck back up and see what was going on. But I didn't want to be bothered. I wanted to get back to cleaning. Had I found my Zen-like space where ideas flow?

Hell no. Not even close.

"See? Nobody home. Front door unlocked, no cameras."

"This ain't my thing," says Bobby. "This is your thing."

"You're here," says Vince. "Help me look. Nothing's going to happen."

"Can't risk it."

Marijuana skunk floats off Bobby like a sticky invisible cloud.

"You gotta be kidding me," says Vince.

"I get the feeling you're setting me up, man. This is a trap."

"You think *I'm* part of some conspiracy? To do what?"

"Were you trying to get me to say something about what I did at the Capitol? Are you wearing a wire? Working for the cops?"

"Holy mother of God," says Vince. "You have officially lost it."

Vince tugs on a pair of blue nitrile medical gloves that make him feel like it's finally time for action. The house isn't all that big—three bedrooms and two bathrooms downstairs along with the kitchen and living room. Vince is surprised there's no jewelry. He remembers the writer guy's wife. She wasn't bad looking. At all.

A set of stairs leads up to an office like a disheveled library. A giant computer screen sits on one of those movable desk gizmos in the "up" mode. Vince parks himself where the writer would stand. He spots a fat black leather wallet on a stack of papers and bills. It coughs up $120.

Vince sits in the guy's leather office chair, shuffles through stacks of folders and magazines and notes. He yanks open the drawers on a wooden tabletop filing cabinet—an antique. Receipts, stamps, blank checks, more file folders, and Bobby mutters a panicky "come here my precious" for the hell of it.

Boom the bottom drawer floats open and stacks of cash sparkle back at him as if to say, "What the hell took you so long?"

Aw, hell.

I had to face facts.

I had trouble.

And there was one big problem.

I hate trouble.

I hate confrontation. As much as I try to inject my stories with conflict, I hate it. My wife once called me a "pleaser."

Is that a bad thing?

Those two had been at my house for too long.

I pulled the ladder back down into the cistern. I was two steps up when I heard the rattle of the dinky orange pickup.

Door number one:

Let them go and find out at the end of the day if they wrecked the house or stole some stuff. The idea that they would find the cash, I thought, was preposterous.

Door number two:

Run out in the middle of the road and insist they stop; hope to not get run over.

Door number three:

Whistle.

I whistled. It's the same piercing sound I use for Arlo

when he's distracted by a gopher hole or a coyote track. It's shrill. For the life of me, I didn't think the whistle would make a difference. But it was a hot day and they had the windows rolled down and maybe the sound gave them a jolt.

The driver braked. The truck skidded badly, probably due to cheap tires or worn brakes.

The way I had the ladder oriented, I had to climb out of the cistern with my back to the road. For a few seconds, I felt vulnerable and exposed. I'm not sure if it was the driver who shouted or the passenger. Arlo, by this point, overcame his aversion to the heat and decided my whistle or the truck noise was enough turmoil to warrant attention. He headed to the truck with his chocolate tail wagging.

Arlo—such a *pleaser*.

"Hey there!"

I shouted it like a friendly country bumpkin.

The guy riding shotgun and closest to me climbed out of the truck. He zinged rapid-fire epithets at the driver. The engine had died, and the driver was trying like hell to get it restarted.

"Hey," I said. "You lost?"

It was the single weakest question I could ask.

"I told you!" shouted the driver, who cranked the balky engine to no avail.

"Told you what?" I said.

Probably figuring he wasn't going anywhere soon, the passenger gave his full attention to me. I put him at five-ten. He was plus-size with long, frizzy dark hair and deep-set eyes. He wore loose blue jeans, a black baseball cap, and a gray T-shirt that might have doubled as a grease rag.

"Nothing," he said. "He thought his buddy lived up this road."

"He doesn't know where his *buddy* lives?"

"Come on, Vince!" the driver shouted.

"Vince who?" I said. "What are you doing on *my* property?"

Now *that* sounded like something a true rural westerner would say.

"Like I said," said Vince. "Wrong turn."

The passenger door remained open. The driver jammed at the key. The driver looked at me from his seat on the far side of the truck. I recognized him. The scraggly hair, the weak soul patch. He was a local celebrity whose 15 seconds of fame involved his participation in the riot in Washington. I'd read articles about this kid—more than a few on websites where he played himself off as more of a radical bad boy than his "just went to observe" pose for the mainstream media.

Bobby Means.

The name came to me instantly, in part because I had been building a character around him in "The Water Novel." But I had found it hard to write about someone who chooses to live in ignorance and darkness. Applying non-logic to words isn't the way I work.

There was something vaguely familiar about Vince, too.

"It doesn't seem like it would take you so long to figure you had the wrong place." I hated the idea of getting in a situation where I would need my Bruce Lee whirl-kicks. I had no such skills.

Bobby climbed out of the Cheeto on wheels. The door squawked. Vince turned at the sound, turned back, said nothing.

Vince's pockets bulged.

"Need a tow truck?"

Vince shook his head. "We'll get it going."

Bobby hung back. His pockets were plump, too. "Give it a minute. It's got to cool."

Bobby Means had one hand behind his back.

"Let's cut the crap," I said.

"What?" said Vince.

"There's no *buddy*. No wrong turn. I recognize *your* buddy. Bobby Means. It will take a minute for the police to put a surname with *Vince*. One trip up to the house and I'll know what's missing and it won't take much."

"Take much to what?"

"To cause trouble."

For a man with zero weapons, a pleaser pet, and a phone sitting a light year away on the seat in my pickup, I found myself using words that suggested I was in charge. My heart let me know of its presence in my chest—and that it would very much appreciate it if my brain could wrangle us all out of this.

"You recognize Bobby because he got his name in the paper, but you don't recognize me?"

"Landscaping crew, if I'm not mistaken. You were the laziest one in the bunch."

"You know how freaking *hot* it was?"

"Pays to finish school." I looked at Bobby Means. "And it pays to know the difference between fact and fiction."

"*That's* what I've been trying to tell him!" said Vince. "Ain't that r . . ."

Vince had turned to mock Bobby to his face, but his face was met with a baseball bat flying smoothly through the air in an uppercut whirl. Vince's jawbone cracked. Blood splattered. Droplets splashed my face. Vince went down like somebody switched off the fan on one of those inflatable dancing balloons. No moan. No nothing.

I thought Bobby would turn his sights on me, but I wasn't his first priority. He set about emptying Vince's pockets.

One-on-one, I still didn't like my odds. It didn't help that my insides had gone queasy at the sight of the attack on Vince.

"You do know you fell for a *story*," I said. "You gave yourself to a mob because someone spun something out of their imagination. And you fell for it."

"Shut up."

Bobby pushed Vince over on his back. Bright red blood dripped from Vince's face. Vince was out cold. He would need the bleeding stopped soon if he was going to make it.

"Stories can be powerful." I took a couple of backpedaling steps to my pickup, hoping I'd accidentally left a machete or loaded Glock within easy reach. "I get it. But you gotta ask yourself if that's the way it's going to be your whole life."

Vince's pockets coughed up more bills than Bobby could fit in his full pockets, so he stood up and shoved some of the cash straight down his pants.

"You must have wondered when the feds came around if it was all worth it," I said. "What if you punched a cop, you know, to feel like you belonged? You could be sitting in prison."

"Shut up."

Bobby picked up the bat. He squared to look at me.

"Your friend needs help."

Bobby shrugged.

"He's going to need help real soon."

"His problem," said Bobby. "Not mine."

"My phone is in my truck. I'm going to call for help."

Bobby took three big steps toward me, lifted the bat. "No. You're not."

I held up my hands. "Fine," I said. "We'll let him die."

Arlo looped a couple of circles around my legs. He was worried for Vince. So was I.

"You didn't really think this through, did you Bobby?"

"This was his stupid idea."

"In a different situation, I wouldn't mind asking you a few questions."

"What the hell for?"

"For a character I'm writing."

"He said you were a *writer.*"

"Don't say it like a bad thing. And unless you're going to whack me too, you don't really know your way out of this, do you? You didn't think this through. Plus my wife should be coming up the road any minute."

"Hell," said Bobby.

"It all starts with the facts," I said. "Like the cistern here."

"What the hell are you talking about?"

"Do you like being yanked around? Being misled?"

Bobby was seething. Maybe all the anger he bottled up back east, when he kept his hands in his pockets, was finally coming out.

"You have to decide if you're going to determine your own fate or get caught up in somebody else's reality, which in the case of your trip was a self-serving fantasy by the guy spinning tales about stolen elections and all that crap." Bobby seemed to be listening. "You need to start with the basics. Facts. Things you can see. Things you know to be true. Like the cistern here."

Vince rolled from his side to his back. His face was a pulpy, bloody mess. I worried he could choke on his own blood.

"The hell," said Bobby.

"You either have water—or you don't," I said. "It's simple. You put a stick down, you can see how much water is in the tank. If you're out of water, you get more."

"The hell does this have to do with anything?"

"You check everything that comes into your world. You start simple, like the cistern here, and you ask yourself if something is true—or if you just want to believe it because it confirms your attitude about the world."

"The president said . . ."

"You're going to give a *president* the power to say anything he wants and you'll swallow it whole? Isn't that the whole point of living out here in the west? Being skeptical of some dudes back east, a couple thousand miles away, telling you what's best for you? How's that make you look? *Us* look?"

Vince rolled over again onto his chest. He looked like he wanted to try to stand.

"Me?" I said. "I'm out of water here at the barn. But the tank got dirty. My wife was cleaning it earlier today and her ring fell off and now we're cleaning it. We know it's in there."

"Ring?" said Bobby.

I stepped to the open hatch—the one without the ladder.

"I sometimes think I'll be able to see the gold glint if the sun hits the opening in just the right way," I said. "See anything?"

Bobby peered over the lip.

I came down close to Bobby, pointed inside. "She was

standing just there." I pointed way inside.

Bobby leaned over to see where I pointed. I stood, stepped behind him, and pushed him down with all the force I could muster. Bobby tumbled into the opening, the bat clattering around. He landed with an ugly wet smack. He howled in pain.

I raced to the other opening, grabbed the ladder, and yanked it up. I doubted he could jump to reach the lip and pull himself out, but I slammed on the lid and tightened two bolts just because. I did the same on the second hatch. I called 911 and ran upstairs to the barn apartment for a towel and ice for Vince's bloody jaw and swollen face.

The cops put Bobby in cuffs and shoved him in the back seat of the sheriff's SUV. They decided on a medical helicopter for Vince, given the shattered bones in his face and the possible brain injury. It was quite the drama watching the giant machine land. Arlo didn't snooze through that.

I drifted over to where Bobby sat. Bobby had broken his arm in the fall and wore a temporary sling. I let him vent.

"Yeah, well," I said. "The power of a good lie, huh?"

Someday in the distant future, he might understand. Maybe not.

As for me, I had a pretty good idea for a story. Or maybe a whole novel.

The son of two librarians, **Mark Stevens** was raised in Lincoln, Massachusetts, and has worked as a reporter, as a national television news producer and in public relations. Stevens is author of *The Fireballer* (Lake Union, 2023) and *The Allison Coil Mystery Series* including *Antler Dust*,

Buried by the Roan, *Trapline*, *Lake of Fire*, and *The Melancholy Howl*.

Buried by the Roan, *Trapline*, and *Lake of Fire* were all finalists for the Colorado Book Award. *Trapline* won the Colorado Book Award for Best Mystery. Stevens has had short stories published by *Ellery Queen Mystery Magazine*, *Mystery Tribune*, and in *Denver Noir* (Akashic Books, 2022).

Stevens hosts The Rocky Mountain Writer podcast for RMFW. He is actively involved in Rocky Mountain Mystery Writers and Four Corners Writers, too. He lives in Mancos, in southwest Colorado.

Stokes the Happy

(a horror-love story)

Cepa Onion

To show Brandon I still have feelings, I decide to comment on the body floating by in the dark swirling water.

"It's naked," I say as we walk, "like all the others. Someone upstream must strip them clean—belts, shoes, shirts—leaving nothing for the rest of us. Even with everything that's happened, greed never dies. Right?"

Brandon sighs, which pushes his thin shoulder blades together like praying hands. I can see them trying to slice through his tired white T-shirt. Weird how I just thought of praying. No one does much of that anymore. Especially us.

Brandon is preoccupied with a fly divebombing his face.

"Right?" I repeat. My temper starts to simmer.

"Sure," he says. "Why do you think we're in this situation, Louise?" He waves a hand, indicating the endless dirty water surrounding the thin path we've been trudging on forever—yet another Colorado casualty of melted glaciers. "I'd rather not talk about it again, okay?"

Ouch. Did my boyfriend just tell me to shut up?

Brandon's attention returns to the fly. He slaps it, splats it. "Finally," he mumbles. He licks it off his hand without further comment.

It's the first time Brandon hasn't stuck out his bloodied offering for me to share. What a thoughtless dick. But I'll get revenge. I'll find a fat, juicy bug and savor it leg by leg, right in front of him. Aren't we supposed to be boyfriend and girlfriend? Where's the humanity?

Maybe humanity is bobbing downstream with the twenty or so bodies we've seen since we left Denver. But instead of joining the masses headed for Colorado's highest point, Mount Elbert, now nicknamed "survival island," we've decided to follow a small group to the mountain town of Leadville.

"They say Leadville's magic. See?" So said the toothless old man who convinced us to go. His trembling hand held out a mostly useless iPhone, still glowing with pictures of a cute little town with the one thing we've all been craving: dry land. "What we need right now isn't Mount Elbert's peak. It's Leadville's magic."

Without analyzing the pictures very closely, which we probably should have done, Brandon and I left for Leadville the next day. It's been weird how few living people we've seen. Sometimes it makes me want to reexamine our decision, but then I get distracted with things like trying to keep myself dry and trench-foot free. Plus, there's the paralyzing, humid heat. Especially after the sun burned through my cowboy hat, rendering it as useful as mosquito netting. Which, by the way, I could also desperately use.

"Can you walk a little faster?" Brandon calls without looking back at me.

He didn't even say "please" this time. His mood is dark. I focus on the sweat dripping down my nose. It dawns on me how ugly I must be now. The last time I saw my reflection, my pale skin was burnt to blisters. My aquamarine eyes were smeared crimson, and my body looked like a scarecrow pecked of its stuffing. That must be why Brandon hasn't turned around or shared his dead fly. He's so lucky he's got more melanin. His skin almost looks normal—for a malnourished vulture. To be frank, Brandon has become ugly, too.

I remember back to when he was beautiful. It was fun to go places with him because everyone threw bouquets of approval at his tall, gorgeous self. Like I was out with a celebrity. I was cute, too, with my long blond mermaid hair and movie-star teeth. Waiters gave us the good seats. Where are all those waiters today? I eye a couple more bodies, wondering.

"C'mon, Louise," he growls. "We're almost there." Could this asshole really be the kind vegan man who could make my heart flutter just by the way he looked at me? Even after so many years together, his eyes would melt me.

Now, Brandon won't even turn his head around to acknowledge my existence. I can't help but take it personally.

Stupid dickhead.

That's when we see an old man with wormy skin. His naked body lies face-up on a flat rock in the middle of the endless swirling water. Unlike the others, he's covered in glistening black bugs. If you hadn't seen these bugs before the world flooded, you might have mistaken them for a beaded ebony gown. For some reason, they avoid the man's smiling toothless face. Such a huge Joker-esque grin. How happy he must have been during his final moments.

"Hey!" I call out. "That's the old man who told us about Leadville."

Brandon jumps into the water and wades toward the body. He didn't ask if I wanted to go with him. What a heartless dick.

Propelled by my anger, I yank off my boots, step in and head toward the bug buffet. Brandon is already shoving insects into his greedy mouth. I join him, and without comment, we gorge ourselves. Like everything else we eat, the bugs taste a lot like fecal matter. But flavor has become irrelevant.

Once we finish, we slog back to the trail. Again, Brandon doesn't help me up or even glance my way as we continue on. Replenished by the food, he seems perkier. His steps are quicker, lighter. "There's supposed to be cattle where we're going."

Wow. Almost a conversation. I resist the urge to remind him of how he had once been such an avid animal lover—that he couldn't even hurt a fly. Instead, he'd cup them gently in his hands and transport them outside. It's a sweet memory, but it would have been cruel to bring it up—just another reminder of how far he's strayed from his former self. Brandon's light mood feels tenuous, and I don't want to mess with it.

"Why do you think the old man had such a big smile on his face when he died?" I walk a little faster to keep up.

"Don't know."

"Maybe he saw a fish." I can't let this go. The old man's big smile was creepy.

"Maybe."

"Or maybe he got to magical Leadville, and he wanted to go back to Denver and preach about it."

"Doubt anyone's that dumb."

"He'd be doing it because he was *nice*, not *dumb*."

"Being nice can make you dumb. Ever notice?"

Brandon has a point.

"C'mon. It's just around that rocky hill." Brandon checks his stained, crumpled map. All we have now are paper maps. Long gone are the days of Siri spoon-feeding us directions. No internet. Just water. And maybe Leadville, the tiny town that managed to save itself and remain unscathed. If Brandon says it's around the bend, then why does everything look the same? Three more naked corpses float peacefully by. Their flesh is picked to the bone. But their faces remain intact, grinning big, unnatural watermelon smiles just like the other two.

The smell hits us hard and beautiful.

"Is that barbecue?" My eyes, mouth, and everything else water at the scent. I have been so parched, I didn't realize I had drool to spare.

"Sure smells like barbecue to me." Brandon is animated, almost spinning. We rush around the rest of the hill and stop. Our path has dead-ended at the edge of a vast muddy lake. A stout woman with leathery skin and twinkling blue eyes approaches us on a rustic wooden raft. Her long paddle scrapes the filthy water as she draws near.

I'm stunned by her size. Absolutely no one is overweight anymore. Yet she's as big as a pickle barrel. This place must be different.

"Well, howdy-ho, new neighbors," she calls out. "Welcome to Leadville!"

In the distance, I hear laughter. Even outright giggling. And children, too? The noises are so foreign they're startling. And carrying those sounds is that delicious heavenly barbecue smoke.

"We're here?" Brandon asks, inhaling the air in greedy whiffs.

"You sure are. I'm the one-person welcoming committee. My name is Charon, just like that Greek fella who ferries dead people to Hades." She cackles. "Ain't that a hoot?"

"Hi, Charon. I'm Brandon and this is Louise. Can we please have some of your barbecue?" He pushes forward, practically climbing onto Charon's raft.

Charon sticks out her oar. "Hold your horses, buck-o. There are some rules."

Brandon is trembling, worse than I am. Thanks to a life of starvation diets, I guess I can withstand hunger better than him.

"We'll do anything," he pleads.

"There's just one thing we ask." Charon sounds so jovial. Like she's welcoming us to the state fair. "I need you two young'ens to take these." She lifts something from a pouch. Clutched in her meaty fist are two large, dried purple mushrooms.

"What are these?" Brandon sounds skeptical. "Drugs?"

"Medicinals. Colorado decriminalized mushrooms years ago. Remember? That's when the good folks of Leadville set up shop. Made us everything we are today."

"No, thank you," we say in unison. After witnessing his brother's drug-induced demise, Brandon won't touch drugs. A bad acid trip during high school band practice convinced me to quit.

"But," I say, "we voted for the decriminalization of mushrooms bill. Live and let live, we say."

Charon sighs. "That's nice, sweetie. But if you don't

take the mushrooms, you can't enter Leadville. It's the necessary ingredient." She leans forward and whispers, "It stokes the happy."

I strive to remember what I learned in my Negotiations 101 class that would convince her. Nothing comes to mind.

Charon shoves the oar in the water and begins to turn the raft around. "If you'd rather not, well, I don't want to keep you. Have a nice day!" As if on cue, more smoke and distant laughter fill the air.

"Wait!" Brandon's pinched voice sounds as though he's been punched in the stomach. "We agree."

Charon smiles a wide, beautiful grin. Much like the corpses we witnessed floating by earlier. She again offers the mushrooms. We each take one.

"Brandon." I grab hold of his arm. "You sure?"

Brandon nods. "We need to eat. And at this point, I don't think we'd make it to Mount Elbert."

I hesitate but decide to play along. I stealthily stash the mushroom into my other hand, then into my pocket, and pretend to chew and swallow. Brandon gulps his. I will stay sober and look out for Brandon. I will be his eyes and ears. If I do that for him, he will have no choice but to look at me with the love he used to.

"Now, that wasn't so hard, was it?" Charon laughs a hearty belly laugh and helps us onto the raft. We float across the water. "Let's start with the nickel tour. Did you know the town of Leadville was founded in 1877? In the late nineteenth century, Leadville was the second most populated city in Colorado, after Denver. Seems like history's repeating itself, don't it?"

The barbecue smell claws at my senses. Brandon is staring straight ahead with basset-hound eyes and a droopy mouth.

"I said, 'Don't it?'" Charon repeats with a bit more force.

"Yes," I answer for the both of us. "History is repeating."

"Like a mastodon in a microwave!" She guffaws at her stupid joke that doesn't quite work. I fake a laugh as she cuts the water with her oars, rowing around the lake. She heads to a shore, turns, heads to another. This goes on for what feels like an hour, never getting anywhere, while she blathers useless facts: the date Leadville built the first post office, its first theater, how everyone used to mine silver.

"Fat lotta good silver's gonna do anyone now," Charon adds.

"I wanna be fat." Brandon gazes at Charon with dull, happy eyes.

Charon smiles, no doubt satisfied the drugs have taken effect. "Well looky that. We're here! Can you see all the people?"

We're still in the middle of nothing. Brandon glances at the murk and nods like a bobblehead. "Yes! All the people!" Giggles swallow him whole, like a swarm of buzzing bees.

I don't see any people. Brandon must be hallucinating. Oh no.

He scans the dark lake. His saucer pupil eyes are as blank as drawings of old Orphan Annie cartoons. "And the official band. So colorful. What's that they're all doing?"

"A square dance, and a pig roast." Charon's smile grows big and wide. "It's a Saturday tradition. Today's Saturday. Betcha didn't even know what day it was, did yeah young'ens?" She laughs again.

I don't see a square dance or a pig roast. Just the same murk. Then in the distance, another raft drifts into view. This one is huge, as large as a suburban backyard. There's a bonfire in its center, and around it, filthy men, women and children dressed in gray rags dance like broken marionettes. No organized square dance there, and definitely no band. I can see something on a grill. Must be the pig. I focus hard.

Brandon sniffs the air. "Ohhhh, I can't wait. Look at the lights, Louise. Like from the riverboat. Remember when we did that? Wow. Everyone's dressed in such wonderful colors. Like us. Look at you. When did we get dressed in purple and gold! Like royalty!" Brandon throws his arm around me. Raucous laughter bubbles from his grinning mouth.

I turn away from his affection, because he's obviously drugged and I need to get a closer look at the roasting animal that doesn't really look like a pig. It seems more like a bear, a big charred bear.

"I love you, Louise!" Brandon proclaims and pulls me back to him, covering my face with drippy kisses. His breath smells like an outhouse. Ugh.

Brandon's eyes become more vacant; it makes me uneasy. Then I notice his mouth. The same wall-to-wall grin as the corpses. I catch Charon's face. She's studying me. I plant a fake kiss on Brandon's putrid mouth and pull back, grinning for my life.

"I love you, too, Brandon." I try my best to sound Happy-New-Year drunk.

"Aww. The smell," Brandon says, turning toward the grill. "Do you think we can learn to square dance like them, Charon?"

"I don't see why not." Charon laughs again, rich and warm. "And you'll both get endless water bottles. You need to drink only from those, all right? That water stokes the happy. Plus it's always clean. No dysentery."

"No dysentery." Brandon laughs. "That sounds like a rock group, doesn't it? Welcome to Red Rocks Concert Under the Stars. Tonight's act: No Dysentery."

Our raft docks against the larger raft. All the wide-eyed, grin-faced people stop their sloppy dance and cheer our arrival. I turn my gaze toward the spit grill. That's no bear. It's a big, fat, naked man. Basting in the open flame. Two smiling blond children turn the spit to ensure the meat cooks evenly.

The people bow down to us as we join them.

"Welcome. Welcome. Welcome," they repeat. Consumed with laughter, Brandon staggers all the way to the spit.

Hair that I didn't realize I had stands up on my neck and back. I am terrified. I force a smile and wave at the others as I follow Brandon across the large raft.

"Welcome. Welcome." All the saucer-eyed smiling people continue.

I stop and peer out over the dirty waters. I can escape so easily. Just a quick jump followed by such a short swim. I can butterfly to the shore before anyone notices. Even Brandon. I take the mushroom from my pocket and cup it in my hand.

"Here's your water bottle." Charon appears at my side, startling me. "C'mon. You must be thirsty and starved. Aren't you gonna eat?" She presses her big face closer to mine. Unlike me and Brandon, her breath smells like Thanksgiving.

"Y-yes. Thank you." I take a small step away from her and study the man roasting on the spit. He also wears a huge face-splitting grin.

I take the water bottle from Charon, positive it's spiked

with mushrooms. I'll have to swim fast. It's so hot and wet that Colorado probably has alligators by now. Not to mention the hungry bugs and snakes. I look again at the small huddle of filthy people. They pile Brandon's outstretched hands with slabs of human meat.

Brandon gazes at it with an unnatural, ferociously happy smile.

Like everyone.

"Louise!" he calls out, moving away from the spit with meat-filled hands. As starved as he was, he has yet to take a bite.

"Louise! Come here. I got you some!" He holds it up to show me. "All for you."

His bright brown eyes lock onto mine. He is definitely looking at me now. I am transported, through the ugly, back to beautiful. Beneath the skin, back to us.

My heart flutters.

Apparently, that old familiar look is all it takes.

I pop the mushroom into my mouth.

"Coming."

Way back when shoulder-pads were in style, Susan Schooleman (pen name **Cepa Onion**) wrote for Roseanne Barr, was a member of the Denver Center Theatre's Playwrights Group, was published by *Self* magazine and *Samuel French*. She then chucked it all for adventures in parenthood. Three grown kids and a retired math teacher husband later, she has begun inching her way back into the business. Her short stories have been included in three Rocky Mountain Fiction Writers (RMFW) anthologies. She was also a winner in the 2019 RMFW Gold Contest.

We'll Always Have Peaches

Ryanne Glenn

I don't remember how old I was when I ate my first peach. And not just any peach—a fresh, homegrown, Palisade Peach. The Western Slope of Colorado is filled with peach stands throughout late summer and early fall, everyone claiming they have the best peaches of the season. Really, it doesn't matter which one you go to. When you walk past the boxes of fruit, you can immediately smell the sweetness of those peaches. Their aroma permeates the air like nothing else I've ever come across, even chocolate chip cookies.

Sometimes, they'd have samples lying out and I'd sneak an extra one, hoping no one would notice. The perfect blend of tart fruit and sweet juice fills your mouth and before you know it, the minuscule bite is gone, leaving you begging for another taste.

A box of peaches never lasted long in my house. Eat a few for breakfast, one after lunch, then a few more for dessert after dinner. When the fruit bowl was empty, I'd prowl around the house, relentlessly poking one of my parents until they made the drive back to Palisade to get another box of those amazing peaches. Finally winter came and the peaches turned to mush and the trees began to fade. I had to readjust my diet. Not only was my summer ending and school beginning, but I no longer had peaches to get me through.

"It's okay," my mom said. "We'll always have peaches next year."

When I was nine, my cousins came up from Texas for a visit, and my grandparents insisted on taking us all to the Peach Festival. As far as events go, the Peach Festival is one of the more boring ones, especially to a kid, but it's a great place for all the farmers and growers to get their produce out to the public. The most popular booths, of course, are the peaches. Palisade had made a name for itself, even outside the Grand Valley. My cousins had heard me and my family talk about these peaches all year, and they were ready for a bite. We bought three boxes, and they were gone in days.

The boxes sat side-by-side on the counter in perfect view of the couch. Every time someone walked by, they grabbed a peach, and whoever was on the couch couldn't help but grab one as well. It was a strange dance, a game, carefully played by each person, though we didn't know we were playing. You couldn't let one person have more peaches than you, but you couldn't be seen grabbing another, in case someone else did too.

When my cousins went back to Texas, the peaches disappeared as well. It was a busy year in the Valley, and they didn't last long. I kept poking around my grandma's kitchen, looking for just one peach, longing for another taste.

"We'll always have peaches next year," my grandma said.

I was eleven when my mom explained we had to be careful with our peaches.

"We're only buying one box this year," my mom said. "They're just too expensive now."

That doesn't mean much to an eleven-year-old. They're peaches. They're *Palisade Peaches* that only come once a year. Who cares if they're expensive? Then again, I didn't quite grasp the concept of money. But droughts and bad weather had caused a shortage. There weren't as many peaches to go around.

To make things worse—at least in my mind—my sister had also discovered the wondrous peach. Up until then, if I liked something, she wouldn't go near it. But my mom finally made her eat a peach, and she fell in love—just as I had. And we had to make a single box of peaches last the entire season.

Each night I ate a peach for dessert, savoring the sticky-sweet fruit and licking the juice off my fingers. Then I snuck small pieces from my sister's bowl. She was too young to notice, and she never ate that much anyway. After the last peach was gone, my fingers traced the bottom of the cardboard box still sitting on the counter.

"We're out of peaches," I said to my mom, hoping she was lying about only getting one box. "And Jilly likes them now too, so I guess we have to get more."

She saw right through me.

"We can always have peaches next year," she said, and she took the box and threw it in the garage.

I was thirteen when my grandma had the idea to can

peaches. She used to do it with her mom, and she still had all the glass jars sitting in her garage. I was ecstatic. Peaches all year long? What could be better?

We bought two boxes to can, but they were different kinds. The peach farmers had begun to plant a few different kinds of peaches in hopes of keeping more alive for the season. One box was just like the ones I'd had in years past. Soft and juicy and sweet. The others were harder, tougher to chew, sourer. I gave my mom a questioning look, but she just shrugged. If we wanted peaches, they were the ones we got.

My grandma brought out a huge pot and told me and my sister to start boiling peaches. Naturally, I was shocked. You couldn't boil peaches, you were supposed to eat them, savor them. My grandma laughed and plopped a few in the hot water for a few seconds. When she pulled them out, all she had to do was make a small cut and the fuzzy skin slid right off.

We worked over the stove all day. Peeling peaches, boiling the sugar solution, sealing the cans in hot water, and everything else. The kitchen was sweltering by the time we were finished. After leaving the oven on for hours, one of the knobs had melted. My mom wasn't happy about that, but my sister and I couldn't have been more pleased. The peaches were sealed and ready to be eaten whenever we wanted, and we still had a few fresh peaches to eat until the season ended.

The canned peaches were gone by November.

My sister and I went through them so fast, I honestly don't remember what they tasted like. They were gone in a flash of sugar and sticky syrup.

"Maybe we'll can peaches again next year?" I asked. My

mom answered with a small smile and a shake of her head.

I was fifteen when we had a very mild winter. It hardly snowed in the Grand Valley, and the Colorado River didn't run nearly as fast in the spring. The day-to-day weather that year was unpredictable. I remember golfing in shorts in February and wearing pants in June.

I don't know a lot about growing peaches, but I know one thing. Peaches are delicate. They require a steady climate.

One week, the temperature dropped far below average. The orchards had already bloomed from the early warmth. The cold spell would kill everything. Farmers went out with blankets and covered their trees for nearly a week. They took warm water and sprayed the blossoms to preserve the fruit. They spread tarps on the ground to trap some of the warmth.

The peach yield that year was dismal. I hardly remember eating them. They were tough as leather. Not quite as sweet. Not quite as juicy. Throughout the Valley, peach stands were scarce. My sister was almost as disappointed as I was.

"Don't worry," I told her. "We'll have peaches next year."

I was seventeen when the local pizza place came out with Peach Pizza. The Hot Tomato was, and still is, one of the most popular places to eat in my hometown. Of course they have cheese and pepperoni, but they also have pesto pizza, pizza with artichoke hearts and feta, and Hawaiian pizza with jalapeños. Their seasonal pizza during July and August is The Peach. Canadian bacon, mozzarella, gorgonzola, rosemary, and of course, fresh Palisade Peaches.

I never thought peaches could taste better than right off the tree, but that pizza was one of the best things I've ever had in my life. I could have eaten an entire pizza by myself, it was so amazing. The flavors blended together in a way that I never could have imagined. And the peaches . . . they were beyond compare. But it couldn't last. They only had so many peaches for each day, and unless you wanted to eat dinner at four o'clock, you weren't getting a Peach Pizza.

Things were looking up. The peach harvest was good that year, and peach stands were once again scattered across the Valley. The peaches weren't as juicy as I remembered, but they were the perfect blend of sweet and tart. When the season ended, the Hot Tomato apologized and changed their specialty pizza.

"The Peach will be back again next year," they said, and an entire town held on to that promise.

I was nineteen when I moved into my first apartment at college. I left the Grand Valley earlier than usual to move in. For me, this meant missing most of peach season. I made sure to have a slice of Peach Pizza just before I left, but for some reason, it didn't taste nearly as good as it had the year before. It tasted empty, and I knew I was just tormenting myself, giving myself a taste of something that I couldn't have more than a few bites of.

Fort Collins didn't have peaches like Palisade. The peaches from the stores were hard and not at all sweet. They claimed to stock "Fresh Palisade Peaches," but they don't know fresh. They don't know the feeling of picking a peach straight from the tree and eating it right there.

That's why I brought a box with me. We stopped on the side of the interstate at a small peach stand and loaded a box into my already bursting car. The entire drive over the mountains, I thought about those peaches. I thought about sharing a piece of my home with my friends. I imagined biting into one of those amazing, delicious, perfect peaches as a reward for the hard work of moving.

When I opened the box in my apartment, my heart sank. These weren't the peaches of my dreams, my childhood. These peaches were small and wrinkled. They were tough to peel, hard to cut, impossible to eat. The nice golden color I had come to expect from a peach was nowhere to be found, and my hands weren't even sticky from the juice. I don't think I've ever been so disappointed in peaches.

I tried to tell myself that it was too early for the good peaches. Maybe the five-hour drive had ruined them. But I knew the truth. I knew how mild the winter was, I saw how little snowmelt the Valley got, I lived through the hot days when rain was nothing more than a dream.

"I'll try the peaches again next year," I said to myself, still not really believing I'd ever have the perfect peach again.

A haze covers the Grand Valley this year, and I don't think anyone really knows what it's made of. Most of it's smoke—from the uncontained wildfires that rage across the state. Lakes and reservoirs have been drained till there's nothing left but cracked dirt. The trees are so dry, even the smallest spark causes a blazing fire that consumes acres of once-beautiful land. The Colorado National Monument is nothing more than a blurred outline, and the Grand Mesa is lost in the smoke and haze.

I haven't actually had a peach this year. Sometimes I'll see a small stand on the side of the road as I drive to work, but even they only have a small folding table with three or four boxes. In a way, I'm almost scared to try a peach now. Because what if that memory of sticky-sweet juice running down my chin as I bite into the soft flesh of the sweetest thing I've ever tasted is nothing more than a dream?

Maybe . . .

Maybe we won't always have peaches.

Ryanne Glenn started writing short stories when she was ten and was first published in Fruita's local newspaper. She took her first creative writing class in high school, and was inspired to expand her writing into poetry and longer stories. After struggling with depression in her first year at college, she turned back to writing as a healthy outlet for her emotions. She wants to write strong female role models and is excited to share her stories with the world.

Ryanne works in Denver for a digital pathology company. She loves to golf, though after playing for twelve years, her handicap should be much lower than it is. Between writing and work, she often visits her hometown of Fruita, Colorado to spend time with her family and dog, Captain Carl.

A Blip in Time

Pat Stoltey

The wife and kids, and even the dog, were gone for a long weekend. I had four days to myself. Four days and five nights alone in Blancherton, Colorado, to finish my novel. I'd promised to keep my phone turned on until the whole family was safely inside at Grandma's house. After that, I was off the grid until the family headed home early Tuesday morning.

While I waited for the safe arrival call, I set up my laptop on a table next to my favorite chair, gathered snacks and bottles of water to reduce trips to the refrigerator and pantry, and added a notebook and a handful of pens. Final checks of my email and social media accounts came next, followed by a review of news headlines and the stock market to make certain all was well in my universe.

My wife, two kids, and Hal—a three-year-old pit bull/poodle mix, don't ask—were my heart and soul, but for this weekend, I couldn't be happier to have them out of my hair.

After hearing my family was safe in Aspen, I was able to turn off, shut down, disconnect, and unplug. When I finished, I had nothing on my laptop screen but a page titled Chapter Thirty-Six followed by white open space. A nearly blank page to fill with the next scene in a mystery about a novelist who's stalked by a crazy fan. It's nothing like Stephen King's *Misery*, though. In my story, it's the crazy fan held captive to write endless rave reviews for my protagonist's books.

After thirty minutes sitting in front of that almost blank page, I opened a box of crackers and munched away as I stared at the white space not filling with words.

I'd made it thirty minutes without the phone and the internet, though. That was quite an accomplishment in itself. The clock on the end table said it was 8:40 Friday morning. Clearly, I hadn't had enough coffee to get my brain moving. My muse was still asleep. She probably needed coffee. And a croissant. She's a French muse. Dresses in a cute maid's outfit and whispers in my ear.

Never mind. That has nothing to do with what happened next.

The doorbell rang. We have one of those doorbell cameras, but it's hooked up to my phone, which, as I already mentioned, was turned off. Ignore it and they'll go away.

That did not happen. The doorbell rang again and again. Then the knocking started. First lightly, then a pounding that pissed me off. I set the laptop aside, jumped to my feet, and stomped to the door. I flung it open. "What do you want? Can't a man have a little privacy in his own home?"

The two people at the door wore uniforms that had BLIP embroidered across the pockets. It's never good to yell at a person in a uniform.

"Sorry," I muttered. "I was busy and—"

"Are you John Whipperly?" the BLIP woman asked.

"I am."

"Are you okay?" the BLIP man asked. "We were alerted that you went dark."

"You can see I'm fine. Who alerted you? Went dark? What does that mean?"

The BLIP man frowned, apparently annoyed by my ignorance. "Not a who, a what. When a person goes dark, we're required to investigate. The signals stopped, you see. Have you had a power failure?"

"What are you talking about? Who requires you to investigate?" I pointed to the embroidery on the man's shirt, not daring to point at the woman's chest. "What is BLIP?"

"You don't know about Local Ordinance 732459A27?" She turned to the man. "Another one who doesn't stay informed."

"What is Local Ordinance . . . whatever you said?" I asked, a big sigh ready to deliver after hearing about this latest invasion of my privacy. Will it never stop?

"I'll explain, but first answer my question. Have you had a power failure? That gets you a pass for the first offense."

"No, no power failure. I'm a writer with a long weekend to myself, and I'm trying to finish a novel. Turning everything off is how I stay focused."

"I see, and yes, I do understand," the BLIP man said, drawling the words out slowly as though he wasn't quite prepared to tell me the rest of what he had to say. "You should know by now, that's not allowed."

"Because of Local Ordinance 732459A27," added the BLIP woman.

I shook my head and adopted a mouth-open, eyebrows-raised, stupid expression, as near as I could tell because I couldn't see my own face, but I had a pretty good feel for weird facial contortions. Writers study that stuff, you know. Occasionally I go to a coffee shop or the mall to observe body language and eavesdrop. But again, that has little to do with my story.

I finally let the sigh go and asked again, "What is that local ordinance thing and what is BLIP?"

The BLIP man bowed his head for a moment, apparently gathering his thoughts. Then he looked up and recited what must have been the full text of the local ordinance. It went on and on forever, most of the legalese floating somewhere between his face and mine while I tried to catch the gist of this new law intended to keep track of everyone in the town of Blancherton.

The words I caught fell into place as "No one is allowed to evade the tracking devices under penalty of prosecution. This ordinance will be enforced by the Blancherton Location Identification Police whose members may chastise or punish offenders where the evasion is deemed to be intentional."

"I didn't know," I stammered. "When did this happen? I didn't hear anything on the news."

"The ordinance was passed last Monday and made effective immediately," the BLIP man said. "I'm sure you know that ignorance of the Ordinance is no excuse."

"This ordinance is less than a week old and there's already a special police unit?"

"Indeed," the BLIP woman said. "We're very proud of the rapid response. This is a way to find lawbreakers trying to escape police surveillance and to protect law-abiding members of the community."

"Well, I'm obviously not running from the police. I just want a long weekend of total quiet with no distractions so I can finish my book."

"Yes, but that's not allowed."

"I'm not allowed to write a book?" My voice squeaked

with indignation, even though I knew that's not what the BLIP woman meant. Writers are also very good at twisting words and ideas to confuse the reader, or in this case, the listener.

"You're not allowed to disconnect from the world," she said. "Let me refer you back to Local Ordinance—"

"Fine. What device do I have to reconnect in order to avoid interruption?"

The BLIP woman nodded. "Anything will do. Your Home Assistant. Smartphone. Sign on to one of your message or shopping accounts. You must, however, open a browser that allows tracking."

"I'll do that. Are we finished here?"

The two BLIPs paused, then the woman said, "There's one more thing we need to do. As you heard in the ordinance, we have to write you up and file this first warning in your record. Subsequent offenses will have more serious consequences."

Stunned, I tried to recall that chanting recitation of the ordinance by the BLIP man and got nothing back but the droning sound of his voice with the occasional words I'd remembered.

I had to get rid of these creeps in a hurry. "I'll turn on my phone," I said. "Will that be okay?"

"Absolutely." The BLIP woman nodded at my sudden capitulation as she handed me a copy of the warning that would go into my record. "Or you can activate your Home Assistant." She glanced at her clipboard, then revealed that she knew the inner workings of my household. "You have Home Assistant Felicity, right?"

"Right."

"That would work as well. We can monitor anything

these days."

I closed the door as soon as they turned their creepy backs.

Finding my phone was the first challenge. Being forgetful was only one of my problems when I bounced out of writer mode and back into real-life mode. Absent-minded, confused, prone to babbling and wide-eyed lapses in attention, I'd slowly transition from my fictional world. Now, after the abrupt removal of my stare-down with the almost-empty white screen and the shock of hearing I was being monitored by the town of Blancherton, I wandered around the house in search of the phone in unlikely places.

I finally spotted its charging cord plugged into a kitchen outlet and discovered the phone behind the toaster. The phone began pinging at me the second I turned it on. I hated pinging but had never bothered to kill the action or the sound. There was no time to mess with that now. I unplugged the charger from the wall and took the phone upstairs to the bedroom, placed it on the bed, and piled pillows and blankets on top.

Once back downstairs, I couldn't hear the phone at all.

With another long-suffering sigh, I returned to my laptop, brought the monitor back to life, and once again stared at the almost-empty white page.

Thirsty. A glass of water and a cup of coffee would help. A handful of trail mix. Oops. More water.

Back in the chair, my fingers hovered over the keyboard, I let my mind wander back to my story. What should happen next?

Actually, what had happened in the last chapter? I could not, for the life of me, remember the last scene. I paged-up to the beginning of Chapter Thirty-Five and started to read.

The doorbell rang. And rang again. And again. Then the knocking.

I ran to the door, threw it open, and had a screaming, "What?" on the tip of my tongue. Then I bit my tongue without speaking. It was the BLIP woman, alone this time.

"I forgot to tell you that we'd be calling once you turned on the phone. You are required to answer."

"You said I only had to turn it on. I still don't want to be bothered, so I put the phone upstairs where I couldn't hear it."

"Sorry. But you'll have to answer when we call. It's in Amendment II of Local Ordinance 732459A27."

"Why?" I cried. "Why isn't it enough to have the phone on?"

"You could have the phone turned on and still be in danger," she said. "What if you fell down the stairs and broke your back? How would we know that? What if a killer broke into your house and shot you but left your phone sitting on the table, turned on and totally pingable? Local Ordinance 732459A27 is intended to protect our good citizens as well as track criminals. A BLIP in time saves lives."

"Fine. I'll keep the phone down here, and I'll answer when you call."

"Very good, Mr. Whipperly. You have a nice day."

After calling me once an hour for the rest of the morning, the BLIP calls tapered off. They didn't call again until after mid-afternoon. Unfortunately, everyone else in my universe had my number and the pings were never-ending. By mid-afternoon, I'd read all of Chapter Thirty-Five, decided what the next scene should be to open Chapter Thirty-Six, and filled one page with mindless drivel that would never survive my next edit.

Beer. I needed a beer. Maybe six beers. Then a nap.

A thought. Could I get away with turning off the phone at bedtime? If so, I could write all night and let the phone ping me to death during the day.

Another thought. What if I turned on my Home Assistant Felicity instead of my phone, then set a digital recorder on a loop to ask questions and give occasional instructions? I could take my laptop upstairs, or even to a coffee shop, and no one would be the wiser.

An hour later, I settled into my favorite corner of the Koffee Klatch Koffee Shop and fired up the laptop. First things first, disconnect the WiFi connection. Second, open the file containing my novel. Third, stare at the mindless drivel under the words Chapter Thirty-Six. I deleted everything except the chapter title.

"Are you John Whipperly?"

Startled, I looked up to see the BLIP woman standing too close to my elbow, peering over my shoulder as though to see what was on my screen. I closed the laptop and scooted my chair to the side to put more space between us.

"You know I am. You were at my house this morning."

"Are you okay?" the male voice came from behind my back.

A shiver raised the hairs on the back of my neck. I scooted my chair farther to the side and looked up at the BLIP man.

"We were alerted that you went dark," he said.

"But I left Felicity on." I started to add an explanation of the digital recorder communicating with Felicity. *Better not*, my darling little French muse whispered. I bit my tongue and waited to see what the BLIPs would say next.

"Felicity did not detect body heat in your home. She alerted us that you might be dead. A BLIP in time saves lives."

"How did you find me here?"

"Your laptop," the BLIP woman said, nodding at my closed computer. "The second the WiFi connects, our system is pinged. That would have been fine, except the pinging stopped and the system sent out an alert that you might be dead . . . or intentionally evading detection."

"I didn't know," I mumbled. "The only reason I turned off the WiFi is to avoid distractions while I try to finish my novel."

"I see, and yes, I do understand," the BLIP man said, drawling the words out slowly just as he had done at my home. "You should know by now, that's not allowed."

"Because of Local Ordinance 732459A27," added the BLIP woman.

What the hell? This sounds like an instant replay of the conversation at my house.

I shook my head and adopted the same mouth-open, eyebrows-raised, stupid expression I'd tried for earlier in the day. I could play that game, too. I sighed and asked, "What is that local ordinance thing and what is BLIP?"

The BLIP man bowed his head, then he looked up and recited the local ordinance, in the same way he'd done that morning, ending with, "This ordinance will be enforced by the Blancherton Location Identification Police whose members may arrest and detain offenders where the evasion is deemed to be intentional."

The BLIP woman took a step nearer to me, so that our knees were less than an inch apart. "Is your evasion intentional, Mr. Whipperly?"

I scooted my chair back. "Of course not!"

She took a step closer. "Then you will connect to the local WiFi immediately?"

I flipped open the laptop and reconnected, my hands shaking just a little as I tried to figure out what the heck was really going on here. "Okay, it's done. Are we good?"

The BLIP woman took one step back, then another. For a couple of seconds, the two BLIPs stood and nodded. Together. They were nodding in concert. I'd never seen anything so chilling in my entire life.

Finally, the BLIP man said, "Very good, Mr. Whipperly. You have a nice day now. And good luck finishing that book."

These people are so weird. One would think they're robots.

Then the pieces started to fall into place. The almost immediate availability of an enforcement squad for a just-passed ordinance. The reliance on technology for tracking and harassing. The BLIP's recital of scripted inquiries and the full ordinance text.

I knew we had a research and development plant just outside town that was rumored to be working on artificial intelligence. Were the passing of this ordinance and the creation of these BLIP characters related? I was in a coffee shop full of people. Was I the only one stalked by a couple of BLIP robots?

I shut down my laptop, grabbed my coffee, and hurried out the door. The BLIPs were standing next to an SUV with tinted windows. There was a shadowy figure in the driver's seat. The visor was pulled down so I couldn't see much, but it appeared the driver also wore the BLIP uniform. Practically tiptoeing, I walked up behind the two BLIPs who'd called on me twice that day and poked the man in the back. He didn't respond, but before I could say anything, the side door of the SUV slid open and the BLIPs climbed inside.

Determined to get to the bottom of this insanity, I stomped to the driver's side and knocked on the window. It did not open. The side door slid shut with a whoosh and a click. The vehicle pulled away while I stood there fuming. The SUV did indeed have Blancherton Location Identification Police stenciled on the driver's side door.

I got into my car and drove home, fired up the computer again, and did a search for Blancherton Ordinances. I couldn't remember the full number the BLIPs had recited so I scrolled through every entry for Blancherton's city council meetings and every law or order passed in the last two years. There was nothing about location identification.

Noting the number to call for city information, I tried the direct approach. After an hour, I gave up. I can only sit so long waiting through the continually repeating message that my call is important and will be answered by the next available representative.

There were options. I could drive to City Hall and try to find someone who knew what I was talking about, but I had a sneaking suspicion that was a blind alley. I had a better idea.

The first step was to go off grid again. I went through the whole house, turning off Felicity, the digital recorder, my phone, my laptop. Just to be absolutely sure, I unplugged the router. Then I sat down to wait.

In less than thirty minutes, someone knocked at my door. The same two BLIPs stood there. The BLIP woman spoke first. "Are you John Whipperly?"

I grabbed the BLIP man and yanked him inside the door. He fell to the floor, his arms and legs akimbo.

"Are you John Whipperly?" he asked. Then he repeated it again.

I turned back to face the BLIP woman. "Are you John Whipperly?" she asked.

"Yes, I am."

"Are you okay?"

I grabbed a hunk of her uniform right at chest level and dragged her inside, slamming the door shut. She stumbled as I gave her a shove, then toppled to the floor.

I sat down to observe the BLIP folks. They never moved. After a few minutes, there was another knock at the door. I didn't answer. The knocking was repeated at intervals for thirty seconds or so. Then a loud voice: "Are you John Whipperly?"

I didn't answer.

The next thing that happened scared the living crap out of me. The front door crashed open and a big, burly man wearing the BLIP uniform marched inside. "Are you John Whipperly?" he asked.

I jumped to my feet. "Yes, yes."

"Are you okay?"

I couldn't stand it. Really? The BLIP minder was also a robot?

"Yes, I'm fine."

"It is a punishable offense under Local Ordinance 732459A27 to harm anyone working for BLIP."

"Punishable? How?"

The burly BLIP pulled something that looked like a tiny stun gun from his pocket. Before I could react, he grabbed my arm and zapped me just above my wrist.

"What the hell was that?" I yelled.

"Offender microchip." He grabbed the BLIP man and woman by the collar at the back of their necks and set them upright. "Transport," he told them. Then all three walked out the front door to the SUV and climbed inside.

They were gone, but I was left standing at my smashed-in front door in shock. My arm stung where the creep had hit it with the zap gun. I examined the little red spot carefully, unable to believe I was now microchipped and branded an offender of some kind. It occurred to me that I could try digging around the spot to see if I could pry the chip out, but frankly, I'm not good with cutting on my own body. Head for the emergency room for an X-ray?

No, I decided. There's no point in making trouble. Instead, I went through the whole house, turning on every device I had, including the television. Then I went into the closet and searched through the box that contained a few old gadgets. I retrieved my sound-blocking headphones and placed them securely over my ears.

I sat down in front of my computer and once again opened the file to Chapter Thirty-Six.

A message box opened on my screen. *Answer your phone.*

I sighed and picked up my phone, moved the headphones aside to put the phone to one ear.

"Is this John Whipperly?"

"Yes, it is."

"Are you okay?"

"I'm fine. Every device I own is turned on. My body is right here in my chair, so my body heat should record on your sensors. What is wrong now?"

"Yes, your phone is on. You are required to answer when

we call. It's in Amendment II of Local Ordinance 732459A27."

"Fine, I've answered. Are we good?"

"Yes."

"May I get back to work now?"

"Yes, of course."

I disconnected the phone, replaced my headphones, and once again stared at the blank page titled Chapter Thirty-Six.

A message box opened on the screen. *Click here for the full text of Local Ordinance 732459A27.*

I couldn't close the message box without clicking on the link, so I clicked. Instead of the Ordinance, however, a full-screen website called EXPERIMENTS IN AI opened with a couple of laughing robots dancing across the top of the screen.

The explanation of the site and the experiments followed, basically explaining that Ordinance 732459A27 and BLIP were fictitious, there was no microchip in my arm, and that I had been targeted for the experiment because of my tendency to go offline and deprive all those big tech companies of my unwilling participation in their tracking and advertising goals. The website didn't use quite those words, of course, as they tried to make it all sound like a wonderful project to provide Blancherton citizens with a deeper level of safety than we could provide on our own. At the bottom of the page was an apology for any inconvenience the experiment had caused and an assurance that my part in the experiment was now concluded.

There was no phone number to call. No email address. No physical address. Not even a post office box. While I sat there studying the site and rereading parts of the bizarre explanation, the whole site slowly dissolved, and I was back to my blank page titled Chapter Thirty-Six.

Thank God! I jumped up and trotted through the house, turning off everything electronic except my computer. I disconnected my WiFi, turned off my phone, and sat down with a huge sigh. At least the bizarre events of the day had given me an idea of where to take my fictional author and his captive reviewer.

Stanley started typing again, I wrote, *his full focus on the novel's last page. He'd make his editor's deadline with time to spare. Just then, there was a knock at the door. Stanley gritted his teeth.*

I felt that little surge of joy that comes with putting words on a blank page. Finally!

Then someone pounded on the door jamb. I got up to see who was there.

The BLIP man and woman stood on my stoop. "Are you John Whipperly?" the BLIP woman asked.

What's this? A glitch in the program? These BLIP characters haven't received the "stand-down" order?

"Yes, I'm John Whipperly."

"Are you okay?"

"No, I'm not okay. I'm dead." Ha, that was not an expected answer in their stupid little program. The two BLIPs stared at me for a moment, then returned to the SUV and climbed inside. The SUV drove away.

I returned to my computer and refreshed the screen. A new message box covered my Chapter Thirty-Six page. It apologized for the recent misinformation about BLIP posted by a hacker. Ordinance 732459A27 is real, the box said. The next lines sent a chill down my spine.

If you are John Whipperly, please report to the BLIP office immediately to confirm your death.

Pat Stoltey is the author of five novels originally published by Five Star/Cengage: two amateur sleuth, one thriller that was a finalist for a Colorado Book Award in 2015, the 2017 historical mystery, *Wishing Caswell Dead: a Sangamon Novel*, which was a finalist for the 2018 Colorado Book Awards, and *In Defense of Delia: a Sangamon Novel* published in 2022. Her short story, "Good Work for a Girl," appears in the 2019 *Five Star Anthology*, *The Spoilt Quilt and Other Frontier Stories: Pioneering Women of the West*. Pat lives in Fort Collins, CO, with her husband Bill, Scottish terrier Sassy, and brown tabby Katrina (aka Katie Cat).

You can find Pat at patriciastolteybooks.com or on facebook.com/PatStoltey.

About the Editors

Paul Martz is an award-winning science fiction author, technology blogger, and former punk rock drummer. His stories have appeared in *Uncharted Magazine*, *Amazing Stories*, *Magnets and Ladders*, and RMFW's 2020 anthology *Wild: Uncivilized Tales*. He has been a member of RMFW since 2018.

At age six, he saw *2001: A Space Odyssey* on the big screen, which led him to a collection of Clarke's short stories—and a lifelong insatiable appetite for mind-bending science fiction. Paul is blind from retinitis pigmentosa. He blogs at AppleVis, a website for blind Apple users.

You'll find Paul in Colorado, sipping coffee while the snow sublimates. He is still trying to teach his cat to play drums. Follow him at PaulMartz.com.

L.V. (Linda) Ditchkus is the award-winning author of the *Sasquatch Series* and *Chrom Y Returns*. Her short story "Opera Without Arias" was included in the 2022 RMFW's anthology *Bizarre Bazaar*. She is honored to serve as the President of the Central Colorado Writers organization. To deepen her understanding of what makes books and stories stand out, Linda judged the 2022 Self Published Science Fiction Competition and Central Colorado Writer's 2023 and 2024 youth writing competitions.

When she's not writing, Linda leads adventure travel trips for the Colorado Mountain Club and travels with her husband. She's been to about 100 countries and hiked or climbed in many of those. She lives an uncomplicated life (without plants or pets) above 7,000 feet in the Colorado Rockies. You can follow her at LVDitchkus.com.

Made in the USA
Middletown, DE
11 June 2024

55467517R00116